An Older Woman Loving a Younger Man

The Story of Two Souls Becoming One
(His and Her Viewpoints)

Bradley Preston and Maureen Preston

PublishAmerica
Baltimore

First printing

PublishAmerica has allowed this work to remain exactly as the author intended, verbatim, without editorial input.

ISBN: 1-60703-192-2
PUBLISHED BY PUBLISHAMERICA, LLLP
www.publishamerica.com
Baltimore

Printed in the United States of America

Table of Contents

BRAD'S VIEWPOINT

Foreword

…as I sat there on my Victorian bed contemplating the future, I began to have some meditative, intuitive thoughts. I was immediately told in my intuition that this was not my imagination. I had always had a vivid imagination, but this was straight from the creator himself. "In the near future, I would meet a blonde haired, blue-eyed man who wore glasses. He would become the love of my life and would take care of me for the rest of it. This was in the spring of 1998.

At once, I called my friend and said to her "I need to confide in you what just came through to me intuitively in my spirit." I announced the information to her and said I knew that it was not my imagination because I've never been interested in blonde haired men. I also knew that he would be much younger than me…

Introduction

After being together for eight years, Brad and I decided to collaborate on a book about our unusual relationship. We thought to ourselves what better way to explain our many differences than to write a book about it. Especially there being 29 years difference in age. Having been diagnosed with macular degeneration earlier, I had begun to lose my vision. This was terribly depressing to me. If it hadn't been for my husband's faith and love I could never have even started this book.

Wanting to express my viewpoint became an almost daily challenge. I prayed "let me finish this book before I lose my site." I want to let the whole world know, especially seniors alone in the world, that "no" you don't have to be alone and "yes" you can love again—despite some popular opinions.

I had always been attracted to younger men, even before I thought there could be a future where someone younger. Brads love has changed me from a shy introverted lady into a career woman interested in changing people's viewpoints about age difference. Does life begin at 40? For me, changed to life began at 60. I often wonder what my mother and father would have thought of our age difference.

I had a new lease on life. Our relationship and this book became alive and vibrant to me. Giving me hope and revealing to me many new avenues that my life could travel down. It brought me to the realization that life truly is what you make it...

Our intention is to share our relationship with the world in the hopes that younger men and older women alike can benefit from our experience and not have to undergo many of the growing pains that we went through as we grew together.

MAUREEN'S VIEWPOINT

Chapter One
Growing Up and Beyond

I grew up in a very unusual household. My mother was an Irish Catholic, my father a Jewish man from Romania who came to America through Ellis Island in New York.

Coming to America at an early age my father was brought up by his Jewish father who was a cantor in a synagogue. They settled in the Detroit suburbs.

My father soon found that he had a talent for singing like the old favorites. Many of the older crowd will remember them. My father's voice was intense and almost identical to the old masters. My father sang on the vaudeville circuit for years. My mother performed in a vaudeville chorus and that's where they met, on the road.

It was a stormy summer afternoon August 15, 1936 when I entered the world.

Being born at home was common in those days. My mother told me it was raining cats and dogs that day and she'd been in labor for 36 hours.

The medicine back then was nowhere comparable to the medicine of today. My mother had no anesthetics or painkillers. It was real labor, and she promised herself she would never go through childbirth again. Wow, did she live up to that promise. I am an only child to this day.

I was painfully shy and ever so lonely as a child. I always wished I had an older brother or sister. Those feelings of wanting a sibling stayed with me a long time.

My parents traveled most of the time and thus I was raised for the most part by my granny from Dublin, Ireland.

I was enrolled in Catholic school from a young age. The strict nuns were my teachers. From grade 1 when I saw my first nun, in their old habits with nothing showing but their face and hands, I longed to be a nun as well.

My desire to become a nun started as a result of my mother's alcoholism, which had been passed down from her mother, unfortunately. However, when I was born my granny stopped drinking alcohol because she knew that my mother would rather drink than to look after a child.

As I look back on my childhood I remember running home from school as fast as I could to try and catch my mother before she went to the lounge to drink. There were no school buses back then so I would run my little heart out to arrive at the stairs, out of breath just as my mother was coming down the steps of granny's house. I would beg her not to go drinking but she would always say, "I'll only be gone a little while Maureen" and then she'd walk off down the street.

I would go in the house and see my granny and ask her why my mother had to drink every day. Each time granny would tell me that my mother needed her space. Of course as far as granny was concerned my mother could do no wrong.

I would go outside and play with the other kids on the block. We played hide and go seek, kick the can, and all the fun games that kids used to play. I distinctly remember stopping each day before 6 p.m. because my mother would start staggering up the street. I would run into the house and hide because I was so embarrassed.

Sometimes I would run down the street, grab a hold of her arm, and we would go to the lane behind the house so I could guide her home and put her to bed. I would have to sit at the bottom of the bed till I could take the cigarette out of her mouth without waking her, after she had fallen asleep. This way I knew for sure that she would not burn the house down. Therefore my playtime with the other kids was often cut short, because I had to look after my alcoholic mother at the tender age of nine.

I remember one of my treats in life was meeting my mother after school downtown at the lunch counter in the local deli. We would have supper together and plan on going to the movies afterwards.

One day as we were enjoying our hot turkey sandwiches with fries the waitress brought us our check. My mom whispered to me "I hope we have enough change for this meal and movies". She pulled out her old, tattered change purse and dumped it out all over the counter in front of us. There were pennies, dimes and nickels rolling all over the counter and onto the floor. I hurried to pick up all the coins as fast as I could. As I finally found the last of them I looked around subconsciously to see if we were being watched. As I expected there were three office ladies snickering and laughing at my mother and I counting all of the change.

Needless to say I was flush with embarrassment and immediately threw all the change back into the coin purse. As the waitress came over to the counter to collect for the check I handed the coin purse and the bill to the waitress and told her to keep the change.

As we walked out my mother exclaimed "oh, I've left my coin purse". She had owned it for years and didn't want to leave it behind. I told my mother "never mind the coin purse, when I grow up and get a real good job I'll buy you a big purse full of coins.

That day is vividly burned into my memory. I could not stand the thought of my mother being laughed at as a child. To this day I cannot tolerate anyone being made fun of whether it is me or someone else. I suspect that these feelings come from living with an alcoholic mother. She seemed oblivious to the psychological damage she was causing me. I doubt it was done on purpose, but the fact still remains that I was scarred for life.

I remember being invited to my girlfriend's houses for supper. I would never accept their offers because I knew I would have to invite them back, out of courtesy. Never knowing whether my mother was going to be drunk that particular night, I would turn down their offers. I did not want them to see that part of my life. So I kept it a secret and went without a lot of my childhood experiences because of her alcoholism.

There were some good times as well. However, my primary memories are of worrying where my mother was, when she would show up drunk, and whether or not my friends were watching. This took a lot of joy out of my life, but it made me a much stronger person in the long run.

By this time my father was a traveling salesman. He would go out for a week or two at a time. When he would come back he would call my grandmother's house, ask for me, and as I sat on that little stool by the phone on the wall in our small kitchen he would ask me where my mother was. Many times I would lie to him to protect her.

Finally he would say to me "meet me at the ice cream shop". I would arrive at the ice cream shop where the most expensive thing on the menu was a banana split for $.25. I didn't want him to spend that much money on me because I knew I would feel that I needed to tell the truth about my mother if he did. He would insist on buying me a banana split. I ate the ice cream as quickly as I could to end the interrogation about my mother. I knew in my heart that the ice cream was a bribe but I loved them both intensely and wanted to protect her at all costs. As hard as I tried my mother never stopped drinking until she passed in the 1970s.

Many of my favorite memories were of nighttime sing-along's with my grandmother. We sat around our old coal stove in the kitchen, where all the cooking was done, and sang songs to candlelight. Granny would leave the door open on the coal stove so we could see the glowing embers of the fire as we sang. We'd sing all of granny's favorite oldies. Then Granny would lead us into some Irish songs. Granny sang tenor and I sang bass. Being directly from Ireland my Granny knew all the good old Irish songs. What a good time we had around the fire.

Saturday night was bath night. The only hot water in our house at that time was in the reservoir on our coal stove. Granny would take the hot water from the reservoir on the stove and pour it over cool water in the aluminum tub. I was basically raised by my Granny due to the fact my mother and father traveled extensively. One must keep in mind that this was the 1940s and things were very different back then. Life was more simple and our problems not so complex. The biggest scandal back then was a woman getting pregnant out of wedlock.

When my father and mother would come home from their travels he did most of the cooking. He had some specialties that I remember to this day. He'd made a dandelion salad that was out of this world. Another of his favorites was eggplant salad. He made some of the tastiest horseradish sauce you ever come across. To this day I cannot duplicate a lot of his specialties.

I recall he would burn the eggplant over the open flames until it was cooked inside and then cover it with olive oil, vinegar and garlic to make one of the tastiest dishes ever.

I was always glad when my parents would go back out on the road. I knew that my father would have to look after my mother instead of me. She never drank when she was with him because he would make sure he didn't stop anywhere near a lounge or liquor store. It was like a holiday for me, I could be a kid again. I came to want to be with my grandmother more and more instead of my mother. My dad would make money in his travels sometimes. Other times he couldn't justify the gas, traveling expenses etc. so he'd come back to my grandmother's house low on funds.

My grandmother and father hardly ever spoke to one another. There were many reasons, none of which makes sense to me.

My father would buy small wares at the wholesalers and then go back on the road. On one of my father's out-of-town excursions, he accidentally found a cottage in a small tourist area. He rented it and we moved there and I began school in a small one-room schoolhouse

19

way out in the country. It was far, far away from all of the bars, lounges, liquor stores, and all my mother's old drinking friends. It was 38 miles to the nearest town, how perfect.

Yet she still found a way to get alcohol. I really enjoyed my new school. It too had a coal stove like the one in my granny's house. There were 12 little desks lined up in the in the same one-room schoolhouse.

At recess time we would all go out and play baseball. It was wonderful to play with my friends and not have to worry about my alcoholic mother. Even though I had to walk home a mile from my new school I loved it dearly. Although I enjoyed my new surroundings I missed my Granny terribly.

Back in those days there were only two telephones in that entire town. One day my mother came to me and said we had to drive to granny's house because she was sick in the hospital.

By the time we got there she had slipped into a coma. She passed away that day. I would've been 16 at the time. I couldn't believe my Granny was gone, I was heartbroken. I felt so all alone in the world. I had never felt that kind of loneliness before. I Granny was the only security that I had for a long, long time and now that was gone. I grieved for months and months. I never really got over the death of my grandmother, but then again that's another book for another time.

Chapter Two
Teenage Years

I had been raised in a strict and controlled environment. Therefore, I realized later, how antiquated my life really was. I was not allowed to go to any school dances, stay after school for gym classes, or any extracurricular activities. So the rebellion welled up inside of me towards my father and I had planned to run away.

Running away turned out to be one of the biggest mistakes of my life. I ran away to my girlfriend's house who was married with two children. Little did I realize that I would become a 24-hour baby-sitter. I found myself in a new and unfamiliar environment. I was told by my friend that I would not be getting paid for babysitting, because I was getting room and board. That left me with no money coming in. Being low on funds, I looked in the paper and found a job as an usherette in a local theater.

When I came home and told my friend that I found this job, she got upset and said I'd have to move out. The theater job, being only a part-time night job, did not provide enough funds to make ends meet therefore, I found another job. This one was a bookkeeping job in the credit department of a well known store. It was their busiest time of year so it worked out real well for me.

I loved the bookkeeping job tremendously, and made friends quickly with a Polish girl, who said I could come and live with her and her mother. We took lunches together all the time.

Everything was going very well until one day when we were at lunch the situation turned sour. She knew a gentleman about our age who had another friend, and they asked us to come and join them. Of course we accepted. There was one major problem with the whole thing, she was crazy over the good-looking one and, unfortunately, he had a keen eye for me.

I noticed him watching me and wanting me immediately. Of course, I kept it from my girlfriend not wanting her to become upset with me. Naturally, I didn't want her to know the truth, because then I would be out of a place to live, again.

I was able to hide it, for three weeks. Until one day at lunch, he slipped me a note under the table. To my dismay she caught the whole act. The note he had slipped me said to meet him at a rendezvous point so that we could get to know one another better. Once she and I got back to the office, she blurted out, "find yourself another place to live". From that point forward we never spoke again.

I met him at the rendezvous point that night and told him what had happened. He, of course, told me that it was not a problem I could come and live with his sister. I was overjoyed, because I had no place to live at that point.

The next day, after work, I went to her house and gathered my belongings. Her mother, having very broken English, tried her best to understand why I was leaving. Not wanting to upset her mother, because she loved me so much, I blamed it on the distance to work being too great and left it at that. How unfortunate life's little meetings and detours can be.

I moved in with his sister Lillian the next day. From the very beginning of this new living arrangement I knew intuitively that I had made a grave error in judgment.

His sister was not working, and had an infant child. It appeared to me that he was fairly lazy and did not want to work either. When it came time to pay the rent, it turned out that no one had any money to pay it except me.

Let's keep in mind here that I was only 17, a virgin, no close friends, no one to turn to or count on, and was now living in their home.

One night my friend came to me and asked me to babysit so she could go out that evening. This created an awkward situation for me because it left him alone in the house all night with me, for the entire evening. All night long he kept telling me how much he loved me and wanted to be with me for life. Of course being of the tender age of 17, I believed every word. He promised me he would secure a job, and unfortunately I fell for that ploy as well.

Before I know it, I had been with John for three months and was now staring a pregnancy straight in the face.

I broke the news to him about my pregnancy. He seemed to take the news in stride, and promised that we would deal with it. The next day I went to work as usual, and found out that I had to work overtime that night.

On my way home, on the bus, I had an intuitive sense-(bad vibes, as they call it), that there was something wrong. As usual, my intuitive sense was right. As I entered the apartment, she was there with her child, and asked me to come and sit down. I noticed he was not there, right away. She tried to be as caring and loving as she possibly could, as she said to me, "he's gone".

Not understanding what she was telling me, I asked for how long. She exclaimed forever. I've wanted to tell you about him for quite some time now. He's no good for you. He did you a favor by leaving, trust me.

Then she told me the rest of the story. I won't be staying here at this apartment, because I cannot afford it. I'll be moving in with my mother-in-law right away, so you'll have to find some other place to live. Would you like to call your mother?

I took her advice and called my mother. Through my broken, weeping voice, I told my mother the whole situation. Naturally, being a loving mother, she said she'd immediately send me a bus ticket to come home. The next day I got the bus ticket, tied up ail my loose ends, and went back home.

Now, you must remember, I begged my mother to keep the last few months secret. My mother and I would keep most of our secrets from my father, especially something of this nature.

I only weighed 98 pounds soaking wet. So I knew that if I bought myself a girdle, which were used a lot in those days, and a couple of crinolines under my black velvet, elastic waist skirt, my father would never be the wiser as to my pregnancy. I was right, he never knew.

He even joked about me eating so much that I was becoming chubby. He finally decided to go away on one of his traveling, wholesale trips. We must bear in mind, I had not been to a doctor and I was eight months pregnant. So I said to my mother, knowing my father would be gone for several weeks, I have got to get to a doctor and get checked.

Neither one of us had a vehicle, nor could we have driven one if we'd had it. We were 60 miles from the nearest hospital, without a car or a way to get there. On top of all that there was 2 feet of snow on the ground, icy roads, and cold, nasty weather.

My mother and I discussed giving the child up for adoption. I reluctantly agreed, because I was so young and naive.

We hired a farmer to drive us to one of my mother friends' house. We left a note at the house for my father saying, Maureen is nine months pregnant and we have gone to a girlfriend's house.

After arriving at our friends around noon and talking through the whole situation, we decided to go to the Unwed Mothers Home because in those days there were no Catholic girl's homes. Upon arriving, they signed me in, and I told them I'd not seen a doctor and I was eight months pregnant. They informed me that a doctor to examine me first thing in the morning. Next, they assigned me a bed, and then they left. Mom and her girlfriend returned to her house shortly thereafter.

Approximately 7 p.m. that evening my father had received our note, called us and said he was on his way. He arrived shortly after 8 p.m. that evening and asked where I was.

When my mother explained to him where I was, he immediately made her take him there. He asked my mother how she could have abandoned me and left me alone at such a time as this.

I had settled down for the evening in an old, Victorian home on the third floor, which was the Unwed Mothers Home for girls.

All of a sudden I heard a banging, and pounding on the front window of the home. I heard my dad screaming through the door let me in, let me in.

Knowing it was my father I jumped out of bed and ran out to look over the railing. As I peered over the railing I saw the head executive letting my father in. She was trying to explain to my father, that it was past visiting hours and all the girls were in bed.

Of course, my father said I don't care, I want my daughter and all her belongings, and she's coming home with me. It was a mistake for her to have been brought here in the first place. As I started down the stairs, he ordered me back to my room to retrieve my belongings and get in to the car. My mother watched and never spoke. We all returned back to Dorothy's house, my mom and dad slept in the spare bedroom and I slept on the couch.

The next morning, my mother and father had decided, amongst themselves that I was too young and immature to take care of this child. Without my input or consent they made the decision for me to adopt the child out. I was not given a choice they made the choice for me.

The next day they brought me to a Catholic hospital and I was admitted. They induced labor after they had administered a sleep aid to me. I was in labor most of the night, but was asleep and didn't know it.

The baby was born in the early morning, and the head nurse notified my parents. They had returned home, so they were some distance from the hospital.

The following day, as the nurses brought in the other baby's', I noticed that they did not bring mine in. So I called the nurse over and asked her where my baby was. She immediately drew the curtain around my bed, came over to me gently softly held my hand, and said to me," they took her yesterday".

I guess I was in shock, because I did not understand what she was telling me. She said to me they should have told you how this works. I said to her, with tears streaming down my face, I didn't even get a chance to say goodbye to her.

They gave me a pill to put me to sleep, and when I awoke my mother was standing there. She asked me where the baby was because she didn't see it in the nursery. Through my wailing, I told my mother that she was gone. My mother was extremely upset that they had not allowed her and my father to at least see their grandchild.

At that point the nurse told me to get dressed, that I was being released. The whole trip home was in silence, what an awful feeling it was. To this day I can't stand it when people say goodbye, because for me it feels like forever.

Chapter Three
A Childhood Wish

Ever since I could remember as a little girl, I had always wanted to become a nun. After going through all of this heartbreak with the loss of my baby, of which I had no control over, I felt even more resigned to join the order of the nuns.

As usual, my mother drank through her entire pregnancy with me. This infuriated me pushing me towards the convent even more. I just couldn't wait any longer.

I found out there was a ceremony coming up at the convent, and I had big plans to speak to one of the executive nun's to get all of the information concerning me becoming a nun. I had many, many questions that needed to be answered, and this was my opportunity. This particular ceremony was the major event at the convent for the year, and would be the perfect time for me to have my questions answered. I knew in my heart that my mother would never quit drinking, and I just couldn't be around it anymore. This was my big opportunity to get away from it all.

I arrived at the convent nearly an hour ahead of the ceremony so I could get a very good seat up front. I remember vividly the music playing in the background it was my favorite catholic song. As it turns out that is one of my more favorite hymns to this day. So, as you can imagine, I continued to question myself whether I was doing the right thing joining the convent at this time in my life.

The priest came out first. Next the girls came out carrying a large wicker basket. In the basket was the girl's hair that had been cut off prior to the ceremony. Also in their baskets were their habit or consecrated clothing, their rosary beads which fit around their waist, and a crucifix they wore around their neck. I tried to take in all of the sights and sounds, wondering if I truly wanted to go through with this.

They all lined up across the front of the church and prostrated themselves before the priests. After all the girls had complied, the priest came to them one by one and said, "What do you ask my child?" Each one replied in turn, "We ask to become a member of this order of Sisters, and further ask to become known as Sister Mary, Sister Jill, Sister Grace, etc. and to be married to Jesus Christ." The priest then said to them, rise up my children, and go out and take on the habit that your heart seeks so desperately. From this day forward you will be known as Sister Mary, Sister Jill, Sister Grace, etc. and not your worldly, given name.

The church was beautifully adorned with large statues of Angels, crosses of gold, large bouquets of flowers from the parents of the girls to celebrate their new beginnings. It gave me chills as I looked around the church and saw all the happiness after all of the loneliness and sadness that I just come through.

As I gazed at the beauty of the church the girls began to file back in and lined up across the front of the church once again.

After they were all assembled, I could hear the parents mumble, "I can't tell which one is my own daughter", they all looked so much different it was amazing.

The priest then began to speak once again. I heard him say, "Sister Mary, known to the world as Jane Doe, you are dead to the world and I now present to you your wedding ring. The priest proceeded to put the ring on her finger while saying, you are now married to Jesus Christ, and for you to leave this convent will require a special dispensation from the Vatican."

The incense was so strong it burned my eyes. The beautiful stained-glass windows were exquisite with the sun reflecting through the glass. It made me want to be part of that ceremony. You could hear rosary beads clanging against the pews as the parents prayed for their daughters.

The awe inspiring choir was comprised mostly of students from the school that I had attended.

The priest then consecrated the ceremony. I remember the candles flickering as the priest went through his motions, as in response to an unknown power about the room. The candles flickered but they never went out.

The reverence of each individual was so apparent that you were almost afraid to speak out loud and break the silence. It tugged at my heartstrings. I felt that this was where I wanted to be. It was without a doubt the most awesome experience for me, and I will always cherish it till the day I die.

I left the convent that day, with a heavy heart, and walked very slowly down the lane way towards my house. The thought that stayed foremost in my mind was of my mother. Once again I became worried who would look after my mother and her awful drinking habit while my dad was gone. This of course would fall on my shoulders, and I knew that to the bottom of my soul.

The months passed and led into years. I felt that my childhood wish would never become a reality. My life continued on and that brings us to another chapter.

Chapter Four
My First Marriage

As the years went on, my mother and I traveled more and more with my father.

My father provided novelty items to festivals, regatas, bingo parlors and the like. My father also engaged in straight sales of jewelry. Me being very artistic and articulate with my hands, I became the jewelry engraver, especially when we would go to the army bases. I was extremely fast and had very good spelling capabilities. My hands, still being small to this day, were the perfect fit for an engraver. My talent was writing very, very small on most any item. They would bring me lighters, rings, backs of crosses, and numerous other objects to be engraved with names and sayings. Most of the time we had people lined up for the engraving for blocks.

One day, as I took a lunch break, I met a man who was giving me all sorts of compliments on my engraving. Of course I was flattered and accepted when he asked me out on a date that evening.

We dated for several months, and got to know one another very well. He even eventually popped the question of marriage, to which I said yes.

We were married in 1965. It lasted 33 years, until he passed in 1998. He passed away in January of '98 from a major heart attack. He had had one previous to this in 1983 and had almost passed on then. For the next 15 years I lived wondering when the worst would happen and take him permanently.

I never knew when he left the house if he would return or not. What a stressful existence it became for me. Many times I'd wake him up after he had nodded off, because I wasn't sure whether or not he was still alive. You can ask any wife who's lived with a heart attack patient for a husband what it's like, it's not easy.

It all started at the end of 1997 when we came home for the winter that year. My husband had not really been feeling well for over six months. As you already know we traveled eight months out of the year, tending to our concessions at the festivals as I had for years with my parents. We decided to take him to his doctor to get a checkup that winter, which, in hindsight, was reassuring for me.

The doctor changed his pills, amounts, and so forth. He told me he could do no more for my husband. The doctor told me his heart was too weak to give him any stronger pills than he was already taking.

By Christmas of '97 he was losing a lot of weight and had almost given up. We went to a club for the New Year's Eve party. Around 11:30pm that evening he said to me, would you mind if we left and went home I'm too tired to sit here? Of course, I said not at all and we went home.

So we celebrated New Year's Eve lying in bed. We wished each other a Happy New Year and went to sleep. On Sunday, he told me he was going to play cards that evening with some friends. I told him I'd be going to church for the evening.

That evening is significant because of the conversation we had in the hallway when he came home. I was almost asleep when he came in and I asked him how he'd done that evening. For the first time in 33 years he said, "I lost". If you know anything about gamblers, (and he was), they never admit to they're loss. I was so surprised I almost couldn't speak. I consoled him with kind words, telling him he'd win next time. His answer took me by surprise once again. He said," I don't think so".

We had never talked about death, dying, or anything like that for either one of us. So when he stood at the doorway and said to me," you know Maureen, if something were to happen to you I couldn't stay alone very long! I agreed with him that if something were to happen to him I couldn't stay alone either. I was flabbergasted at his words. Here he was losing, weight not feeling good at the New Year's Eve party, and losing at cards like he'd never done before. Now all of a sudden he's talking about subjects that we've never brought up in 33 years. We didn't converse a great deal after that and we dropped off to sleep.

Every morning for the past 20 years he had gone and got coffee and brought it back to the house. This particular morning he had not brought the coffee back. It's the little things that you notice.

I had always prayed that if he were to have a major heart attack, it would not happen at home. As I couldn't stand being in that house if it had. As we all know, prayers really are answered. That morning he was in a big hurry, which also was unusual. We drove across town to a Ford dealership and he went in to get parts. I asked him how long he'd be as he exited the car. He said, not long at all.

Perhaps 30 minutes later a girl knocked on my window and asked if my husband was epileptic. Of course I said no. She said he's having a seizure. I exclaimed, "NO!!! It's a heart attack get ambulance immediately".

When I rushed into the dealership he was surrounded by EMT personnel, and I could not get near him. I rode in the ambulance with him to the nearest hospital in Tampa, Fl. All my friends were concerned about me because I had had quadruple bypass surgery in 1995.

I was all alone at the hospital until I called my best friend. She came immediately. Naturally, I was in shock and I couldn't talk for the longest time. So I had my friend speak for me and handle all of the necessary details with the doctors. It was around noon at this time and by 3 or 4 p.m. the doctor came out and told me that he was brain dead and I needed to sign a consent form. It was a DNR form. Do not resuscitate. "If he has another heart attack we will not save him", said the doctor.

My best friend and I talked and came to the conclusion that he would not have wanted to live as a vegetable because he was too active a person.

The doctor explained to me that once someone is brain dead there is no coming back. It took me some time to make my decision, but I finally consented and signed the necessary paperwork. The nurse hung the DNR tag on his bed immediately. We left the hospital around 9 p.m. and went to her house for the evening.

Of course, I didn't sleep much that night, so when the phone rang at 6 a.m. I was already awake. My friend came in and gently said to me, he's gone. It was a Tuesday morning and it was my wedding anniversary. He was gone!!!

The funeral was much larger than I'd expected. So many people that he had worked with for years were there to honor him. We had our ups and downs, but he was a good man. There were 350 people in attendance at his funeral.

Sally, my daughter, arrived for the funeral. She had only known him for a brief time, but loved him nonetheless.

After his passing in 1998 I was pondering those 15 years of stress that I had gone through. It was then that I told myself, I can't go through the rest of my life like that, with all that stress.

I figured it was time I enjoyed myself for a change. Not that we didn't have good times, just that the extra stress that is put on a person, especially one having diabetes like myself, becomes overbearing. So I promised myself that I'd find someone younger than me, so we could enjoy life and he could look after me for a change. But, I'm getting a little ahead of myself now.

Chapter Five
Courtship and Dating

They say that love is better the second time around, and I can attest to that today. There were so many times in my first marriage that life didn't turn out the way I had imagined it would. But, as you get older and become wiser, you look at life in many different fashions.

I feel I must explain how I met Brad, finally. I know you've all been waiting for this moment.

Several months after my first husband's funeral, I was sitting in my bedroom. I began to wonder about my life and my future. Some really heavy, meditative thoughts began to come into my mind. I usually meditated in the evening, or when I was extremely upset. Naturally, I had been, due to his passing. I wrote these thoughts down as they came to me, and then I called a close friend to tell her, because I too, found them hard to believe.

I was told, intuitively, that I would meet a tall, wavy blond haired man with blue eyes, and he would be wearing glasses. He would be much younger than me, 25+ years younger. He would be the love of my life, and would look after me for the rest of my time here on earth.

These are the thoughts that came to me that I wrote down that afternoon. I've had a vivid imagination since I was a child. However, when I heard "BLOND HAIR", I was flabbergasted, and knew for sure it was not my imagination. I have never been interested in blond haired men since I was a young girl. I knew this information was coming from a higher source. So, quite naturally, I began to look for this person. I continued to follow the festival routes, as I had for years.

I had my workers get our equipment ready for the road. We would be heading north in a few days to start our year of festivals. A few days later we arrived in Greenville, North Carolina. The first thing we had to do was look for the location coordinator, so we could set up our equipment. Low and behold, a man was coming across the parking lot towards us, and he asked us where the main office was so he could book his equipment. I was speechless, I could not believe it. There he stood in front of me, a 6'-2" man, with blonde, wavy hair, wearing sunglasses. I knew in an instant it was him. There was no doubt in my mind...I couldn't speak for a moment.

After finding the coordinator, who had known him from the previous year, we were introduced. Time stood still. As we gazed at one another, he bent down and kissed my hand. My knees became weak, my heart almost pounded out of my chest, and I felt a little light headed.

I thought to myself, if I mention to him the thoughts that were brought to me in my meditation, he will think I'm a lunatic. I pondered to myself how I would find a way to make a contact with him. I laid there most of the night, making up all sorts of scenarios. I fell asleep with his face before me, in my mind.

The next day, I woke up earlier than usual. I decided to go out to the festival grounds a little early and tidy up my concessions. I hoped, in the back of my mind, that he would be there. I wanted to get everything organized for the busy day ahead.

I walked over to the coffee shop and you'll never guess who was there. He was ordering breakfast and invited me to join him. I tried my best to stay very calm. Luckily, he was very talkative that morning and carried the conversation, which helped me to remain grounded.

As we finished our breakfast and coffee, and I was dreading our meeting coming to an end, he asked if he could take me to dinner that night. Of course I said yes. He said he'd pick me up around 8 p.m. and he was gone. I had already told him where I was staying for the week.

I raced back to the motel to figure out what I would wear that night, like any woman would have. I selected a blue, nautical design, two-piece, shorts outfit that made me feel very attractive. Of course, I tried it on two or three times to make sure it looked exquisite.

The day seemed to drag on waiting for my date to arrive. I had not been on a date in over 30 years. Around 7 p.m. I did my hair in an upsweep, and before I knew it he was knocking at the door.

The knock on the door made my heart pound wildly. He arrived at 7:45 p.m., and he walked me out to his car and opened the door for me. I said to myself, I knew he was a gentleman.

As we drove away from the motel, he said to me, I hope you don't mind that I took the liberty of reserving us a table at a seafood restaurant on the water.

When we got there, it was one of the most elegant places I had ever seen. It was an out-of-the-way restaurant on a private pier, decorated with ornate, white lighting. It was like a dream come true.

He said to me, you certainly dressed for the occasion. I had selected the nautical outfit, without even knowing where he would be taking me.

Here we were at this elegant seafood restaurant with my favorite music playing in the background. Two hearts that are meant to be together think alike, I said to myself quietly. Now I know what they mean by the term soul-mates.

We enjoyed a delightful meal and I found out that he did not drink alcohol, at all. Of course, I did not either, because of my mother's alcoholism. Quite frankly I abhor alcohol to this day, and so does he.

After we got done eating, there was some more relaxing music playing in the background. What a dream come true this evening had definitely been. As we drove back the 15 miles to the motel, it gave us time to talk and get to know one another a little better.

Finally, he said to me, I can't quite explain the feelings that I have right now. I realize how big of a difference there is in our age, but that doesn't matter to me. I feel like we've known one another forever. He looked into my eyes and calmly asked me if I truly understood what he was saying.

I said to him, before I left home I was told in my meditation that I would meet you. I can't explain what I feel either, but isn't it wonderful that we both feel the same. He walked me to the door of the motel room, kissed my hand once again, and said good night.

We made plans to meet for breakfast the next morning. As we were sitting there, after we had eaten, he suggested we go to my booth at the fairgrounds.

He said to me very quietly, do you mind if I make some suggestions about the set up of your concession. I said to him, all constructive criticism is welcome. He had some excellent ideas to promote sales. After he had explained the new concepts to me, I could see that they would most definitely increase my sales. He even suggested adding some new items, which were ingenious.

My late husband had always been the one to buy all the merchandise, so I truly welcomed his input as it was not my forte. Before I knew it, it was lunchtime. We, of course, went and got a burger together.

Our lunchtime conversation consisted of him sharing with me his many skills, including mechanics, sales, inventory, artwork and design, and the list went on and on.

Understandably, after hearing of his extensive capabilities, I proposed to him a business opportunity that would benefit both of us.

We worked independently of one another for the rest of that week. We would take our lunch breaks together and talk more business. We were fast becoming dear friends.

Our next festival was in upstate New York. We decided to combine our booths into one, large, profitable business. He had all the necessary tools and accessories to, not only build, but to maintain the changes that were being made to both booths.

He designed display racks, showcases, counters, and made some very artistic signs, with lighting, which helped tremendously at night. Having the two combined would be advantageous to us both. I could see that right away.

As I looked at our route schedule, I noticed that we had a bunch of festivals coming up that were by the water. We would also be playing a very large festival in Niagara Falls in approximately 45 days. We would need some inventory that was the same theme as the water.

The festivals we played were generally 10 days in length, with two or three days in between for travel time. So you can see it's a fast-paced life.

We would be going from our current festival to Tonawanda, N.Y., which was next to a beautiful lake. From there we would go to Oswego, New York, then on to Buffalo, and finally Niagara Falls. I suggested to Brad that we purchase some merchandise that had an aquatic theme because of all the festivals we would be playing near the water. He agreed, and we did very well.

I thought to myself, as I watched him coordinate the help, stock the merchandise, and fill the role of general manager, how wonderfully close we had become in such a short time.

We were currently in Niagara Falls, the honeymoon capital of the world. We had talked about moving in together when we got to Niagara Falls, as we were staying in separate motels up to this point. We wanted to see if that part of the relationship would work.

Brad left to go purchase merchandise downtown. I went to go get my hair done. We had decided to meet later for dinner, and find some living arrangements. While we were at dinner, Brad shared with me that he had already taken care of our living arrangements for the week.

Unknown to me he had rented the honeymoon suite at a quaint, little motel just off the downtowns main street. The name was fitting, honeymoon acres.

Our business relationship had become close and personal. It seemed as though our private relationship would need to go to the next level to keep pace. I contemplated whether or not I was ready for that next step.

Chapter Six
Our First Time

As we were having dinner that evening, I thought to myself, he's found another way to impress me.

We had tried to keep the excitement in the relationship by surprising one another. He had definitely surprised me this time. I just didn't know it yet. We drove down the main street to see the sights of the town, when all of a sudden he pulled into the Honeymoon Acres motel. He already had the key to the suite, because he had checked in earlier.

We gathered our things from the car and walked to the room. As we walked toward the suite he made a joke about carrying me across the threshold. He reached down and swooped me off my feet and carried me through the door sideways.

Inside was a pink heart shaped Jacuzzi. There was a full bouquet of roses on the nightstand next to the heart-shaped bed. Tucked inside the roses was the most fabulous card I'd ever seen. Inside it said, to my future wife. I love you, love Brad. He had said to me before, that he wanted the first time to be extra special for both of us. He certainly had surpassed himself on this one.

Due to the fact that it had all been a surprise to me, everything that occurred that night was all spontaneous. The *Jacuzzi* helped me tremendously to unwind and relax. He massaged me, as we sat side-by-side in the warm water together. It was a very sensual experience. One I won't soon forget.

Having been brought up in a sheltered existence it was hard for me to overcome my shyness. However, he was a wonderful teacher and I enjoyed being his student. Did he do some teaching that night or what? Because I am from the old school I won't delve into a lot of the particulars. I would like to elaborate on some of the intimate feelings that we shared that evening, so that those of you out there that think age matters will begin to see how wrong you really are.

Brad was brought up a gentleman in a conservative home. Thank the good Lord for gentlemen. His words were kind. His leather hands became soft as velvet to the touch.

After our Jacuzzi massage, we quietly strolled over to the heart-shaped bed. On the nightstand next to the flowers was a cup of hot water with massage oil in it. He opened up the tube and caressed my entire body with warm oil. It was one of the most sensual moments I've ever had.

What a kind heart this young man has, I thought to myself. And the strong hands aren't too bad either.

We didn't do a whole a lot of talking that night. There were moments when neither one of us knew what to say, so we spoke with our hearts, our eyes and our hands. Minutes lead into hours as our night of ecstasy progressed. We were intimate more times that night then I can remember. Well, actually I do remember them all.

I never realized what being matched sexually truly meant until that night, because I hadn't been up to this point in my life. It went way beyond the physical what transpired between us that night. Our minds touched, our hearts touched, and our souls became one. All of this and the physical too, what a night to remember?

When you find someone in life that's willing to take the time to caress you, and hold you, and spend time with you as though nothing else matters, then I truly believe you've found your soul-mate. That night I found mine.

I had dreamed of this night for many years, but never thought it was possible. I knew that I had made the right decision. I also knew in my heart that choosing a younger man was definitely the best thing I could've done. I'm sure, to this day, that someone my age could never have made me feel the way Brad made me feel that night. And to think he was 29 years younger than me. I don't know what it was about the Jacuzzi, whether the warm water, the jet sprays, or the massage, but it was one of the main highlights of the evening. I still remember it to this day. It was so relaxing, and soothing. It was as if I was the student and he were the professor.

As we lay arm in arm talking of the good times, on that heart-shaped bed, I began to search my own soul and wonder about our future. I hoped that we hadn't rushed into anything too quickly. And yet I knew in my heart that he was the one. It's such a strange feeling to wonder on one hand and to know on the other. And yet that's what I felt that evening.

As the night progressed we were standing on the balcony overlooking a beautiful waterway where three rivers came together behind our room.

The words that were spoken were so honest and sincere. It's hard to imagine it can happen to you, until it does. Truly, words cannot describe our deepest sensual moments. Several words come to mind but, even those don't seem to shine light on the whole picture. Words like amazing Grace, lifelong fulfillment, dreams come true, the bright shiny star, even they don't take in the fullness of what was expressed that evening.

Towards midnight we both felt hungry, so we dressed and found a little Mexican Grill with gourmet chili downtown.

It always seems that your hunger peaks after having an intimate moment or several as it were. Therefore, the food was not only welcome it tasted fantastic. It really hit the spot. This little grill that we had found was famous for very good milkshakes so he ordered me a strawberry, my favorite. He ordered the deep-fried ice cream, which is his favorite.

The Mexican food was a bit spicy but the ice cream was perfect. Brad and I joked about my nervousness during the evening. He told me that he had appreciated my ladylike personality. And that he had wished he'd met me earlier in his life.

We drove back to the motel with my head on his shoulder. What an unforgettable moment. He told me that I was the best thing that ever happened to him and how dearly he loved me and would always look after me. It was as if he was there that day that I was told about him coming into my life in my meditation.

That to me meant a great deal, due to the fact that I'm a diabetic and have macular degeneration of the eyes.

On top of all that I'm a heart patient with high blood pressure. I knew with certainty that we would continue to look after one another for the rest of our natural lives. What a wonderful feeling to find someone that you feel so comfortable with.

Chapter Seven
Commitment

After meeting Brad and really getting to know him, I decided to make sure that he would not be kept in the dark concerning my financial situation.

Money is always important in any relationship, so I asked him one day to drive me to a rural post office. I needed to pay all my monthly bills at that point.

I was already beginning to have trouble with my eyesight, so I let him buy the money orders for me. If I remember correctly at the time the total of the money orders was $3000.

I had been left with some CDs, a piece of property, and some equipment. So as long as I kept money coming in I was fine financially.

I didn't want him under any illusions that we could relax financially and not have to work.

He was also aware that I was a heart patient and diabetic, so it would be more of a decision for him to commit to the whole situation, than it would be for me. The way I look at it, if he knew about all of these payments I had monthly, and he still wanted to commit, then I would know that he was serious.

That evening after dinner I finally said to him," let's talk and level with one another on our future".

I had told him how much I owed on credit cards plus other debts that I had at the time. So over dinner that night I gave him a very large figure, and he never batted an eye. It was as if he knew what he was in for before we had this conversation. He told me he only had a few small debts and that he was prepared to work and help pay the payments. I sat and looked at him in awe. All I could think of to say was, "thank you for your support". I wanted him to know the truth of my situation right from the start. Unlike a lot of women who would not have told him.

Our season was beginning to wind down in October so we decided to go to Colorado to visit his dying grandmother. We made plans and within a week we were headed west. Committing to someone younger than your self is a whole different ballgame than committing to someone older than you.

All of my girlfriends said don't tell him about all your payments you'll scare him off. However, I said to them I want this relationship to be built on the truth not on lies, so I'm going to tell him the truth. As I look back now it was the best thing I could've done for our relationship. It started out on a true note and it's true to this day.

For Brad to say he would help me pay off close to $100,000 in debt was indescribable for me. Once again, I thought to myself, making a lifetime heartfelt commitment to a much younger man scared me a little. But my heart and soul said, don't worry, any relationship sent from a higher source will definitely work out.

I prayed as I always had on important matters and with a reassuring feeling that it was the proper road for me to proceed on I went ahead with the relationship.

I had always thought that younger people were not as good at dealing with budgets and businesses as seniors. I soon found out that was far from the truth. He even began changing the oil in the vehicles and doing routine maintenance instead of me having to take them to the shop which, of course, saved us even more money to pay on the bills.

He would routinely check the air pressure in the tires which kept us from having flats while we were on the interstates. Often times we would make up our own lunches while we were on our long 600 to 800 mile drives in between festivals. Our trips were not always this long, but we did have some big jumps.

We began making some of our own crafts which we used in our booths and this saved us money many times over.

Certain parts of our inventory were quite expensive, but we made our own and stayed to our budget. As each of our business deals transpired I saw more and more that our business plans were working out. The relationship felt right along with it. Again you gain knowledge of one another and valuable experience while working together.

We had combined his youth and vitality with my experience and had made a profitable business out of it. We were together so often that my friends began to call us the Siamese twins. Naturally, I loved it. It's nice having someone that you can count on. Whether young or old when you know someone's got your back the bonds grow very close.

Chapter Eight
Going to Colorado

We came back home to Florida near the end of October. We needed to get the equipment stored on our property so we could go to Colorado to see his grandmother.

I had owned one the property in Tampa, Florida for 15 years at this point. Once we got the equipment cleaned up and stored away, we heard of an impending hurricane bearing down on Tampa. We would have normally relaxed for a week or so before we went to Colorado, but with the hurricane coming at us and the evacuation notices going out we decided to get out of town. We packed up our trailer and headed west.

We left the town that night and headed north on I-75. We had made a habit to travel at night because it's easier on the tires. Anyone that's done any extensive traveling will understand that. We had originally wanted to take 1-10 along the southern United States. However, with this hurricane headed towards the coast we decided to go further north up through Georgia and Tennessee. I don't recall the exact route I just know we didn't get take the southern route like we'd wanted.

We were looking at 2500 miles to go to reach that Grand Junction, Colorado. If you've ever traveled in the fall you know that the changing of the seasons makes the beautiful colors of the trees indescribable.

We got almost 800 miles under our belt that first night. We wanted to get as far north away from the hurricane as we could. At the rate we were going it would take 3 1/2 days to get there. After we got away from the threat of the hurricane and its storm, we slowed our pace a bit, to 500 miles a day.

I watched him drive as I had for the past few months, and the thought occurred to me how lucky I was to have found Brad. It was as if our souls had become one. That doesn't happen too often in a lifetime. I knew that he was the one. I knew I'd be spending the rest of my life with him. Intuition I guess.

As we neared the mountains of Colorado you could see them from a great distance. The mountains were a new experience for me and they became one of my great loves. The first sunset I saw over the Rocky Mountains, I understood what they meant by purple haze. The red rock and other types of rock at that time of year turn purple as the sun sets. It was as though I was in heaven.

The next morning as the sun rose above the mountains I fell in love with that part of the country. I never realized how wonderful the light coming down through the colorful trees could be. It was a scene I won't soon forget.

The solid green evergreen trees against the white aspen trees with all the different colors of the rainbow from the leaves changing is hard to put into words.

The brisk morning was enchanting. You could see your breath in the morning air. The small wisps of smoke coming from the fireplace above the cabin that we had stayed in that night were amazing rising up through the colorful trees. I can close my eyes to this day and still feel and see and hear what I experienced on that mountain that day.

Brad told me of several places that we could go and do some hiking but it would have to be at a later date because we had to get to Grandma's house.

He is from Colorado so he knew the area well. We drove on through the mountains to the west side of Colorado arriving in Grand Junction.

His grandparents had been living there for 30 plus years. Brad had gone to school in Grand Junction so he knew the town well.

We found a small trailer park to put our RV. It was just down the road from his grandparent's house. Naturally we were exhausted from the trip. So we unpacked and relaxed that evening.

The next morning we went to the hospital where Brad's grandmother was being held. She had a chronic cist on her spine.

It is known as Shiringomyilia. It is a disorder of the spine that had made her wheelchair-bound for the past 15 years. She had no feeling from her mid chest down. She had lost most of the taste in her mouth due to this disorder. Every aspect of her life had to be looked after all the time. Although she was struck with this disorder she seemed to be in good spirits.

After Brad talked with a doctor for a short time he came back and told me that they couldn't do anything more for her and she probably wouldn't live six more months

Brad told me he wanted to stay there until her passing. We had not planned on staying there but a short time. So this changed our entire plan. We would have to secure some type of financial income and because it was winter in Colorado our options were limited.

However, Brad came to the rescue again. He informed me that he was a professional glass installer. It was 24 hours and he secured a job with a glass company. There were only three glass companies in a town of 70,000 people and he got a job in one day. It was amazing to me how adept he was.

We visited his grandparents often and Brad got in some quality time with both of them which he had not done in years. Brad's job in the glass industry helped him put in the time. I know it was hard for him watching his grandmother preparing to pass away.

The winter in Colorado was not terribly snowy that year but it certainly got real cold. Several mornings our water hoses froze on our RV. Finally, he went and bought some heat tape, wrapped the hoses and solved the problem. He installed extra panes of Plexiglas on the inside of each window to create insulated windows. It worked like a charm and kept us from using so much propane.

Time and time again he has showed me skills I didn't know he had. Having lived in Florida for over 20 years it affected me greatly being in the cold. My arthritis flared up so I would bundle up in my grandmother's shawl to stay warm during the day. The days lead into weeks and weeks into months. Before we knew it we were staring at January.

His grandmother seemed to be getting better so they released her from the hospital. It wasn't but one short week after that the doctor said her prognosis was not good.

We got a call from Brad's grandfather about a week later, Grandma had passed away. I was so glad that we were there for his grandfather. All the relatives would soon make their way to this small mountain town for the funeral. Arrangements had to be made, paperwork had to be done, and we were there to take the burden off of Howard his grandfather.

It was a tough time for both of us. However, I was glad that we had experienced it together. It drew us closer and closer to one another. He began to lean on me for support which is exactly what I wanted. It was exactly what we both needed at that time.

I had gone through plenty of people passing in my life, but it's different when you're younger and I knew that from experience. Brad had gone through his share of lonely times but now I was there to console him. Our hearts, minds and souls grew closer and closer.

Isn't it funny how life brings you closer together when you truly love someone? I knew now that I truly loved this man, and that he loved me. This incident would bring us closer than any other.

Of course every incident has its downside. I was dreading meeting his family. I was afraid of being put on trial because of the age difference between us.

His entire family was brought up conservative Baptist, and they wouldn't understand the age difference, as was my experience with conservative Baptists in the past.

We were not married yet, they would prey on that, I said to myself. We would have to give them a story to get through this first meeting and the funeral. I loathed the thought of the next few days. It would be a challenge for our relationship, the first and the biggest.

Chapter Nine
Meeting His Family

We had originally planned to go to Colorado to meet his ailing grandmother and we would be meeting his family at the same time. They would be congregating because the doctor explained that Granny would only have two to three months to live.

Brad had been brought up in a very strict Baptist family with a grandfather who was a Baptist minister and a missionary grandmother. Brad's father was separated from his mother when Brad was only 11, due to infidelity. So Brad had to grow up at an early age even though he was the baby of the family. He has one brother and two sisters.

Because he was brought up in such a staunch religious atmosphere we decided to tell part of the truth but not all of it. We would tell them that I was the owner of our business and he was the manager and we were on vacation, thereby, keeping the truth from them because they couldn't handle it, especially with our age difference.

This would keep the questions to a minimum, or so I thought. I was wrong. It wouldn't have mattered what we had said they would have ostracized us like they did, anyway.

After the small funeral at the cemetery, we all went to his grandfather's house for refreshments.

I was treated very cordially by everyone. Even Brad's nieces made it a point to come over, introduce themselves, sit down and chat. I felt especially welcomed at that point.

I thought to myself they are not like most staunch religious people that I've met in the past. I felt as if all would be well. Again, I could not have been more wrong.

We spent several hours at his grandfather's entertaining and visiting. After which everyone went to their respective place of residence.

I felt as if we would make it through this without a big confrontation. We were all to meet later that evening, at the church, for her memorial service.

At this point I had met all the brothers and sisters and their focus, naturally, was on the ill grandmother.

Now that the funeral was over and grandma was gone they turned their focus toward me. Brad and I had caught a ride with his older sister to the funeral, so she was to give us a ride home. I climbed in the backseat and Brad climbed in the front.

Brads older sister had always been protective of him because he was the youngest. As I've already said, there's 29 years difference between Brad and myself. This would be the focal point of his older sister's attack. It became obvious to me immediately that there would be a full interrogation, and there was too. I thought I was ready for all questions. Once again I was wrong.

The older sister seemed the worst. Brad knew that his older sister would come on stronger than the rest because she'd always been protective of him, so he had tried to talk to her to explain a few things about our relationship. She didn't want anything to do with it. She wouldn't have this older businesswoman taking her younger brother away from her. I appreciated her viewpoint, and tried to remain as polite as possible with the whole situation. To say the least I did not win her over.

It was a cold snowy evening as we arrived at the church for the memorial service later that evening. I had on my heavy wool suit, gloves and a hat. As we entered through the side door there were four or five small intimate groups.

Everyone had just lined up for refreshments, and so we fell in line behind them. After getting our plates we headed towards Grandpa's table where his other sister and her two girls were already congregating.

We tried to blend in and join the conversations that were around us, to no avail. We then proceeded over to his brother's circle of friends and family, and once again we didn't fit in. I began to feel completely ostracized and said to Brad, let's try this one more time before we get out of here.

I began to feel as if I were on an island in the middle of the Pacific all alone. Being very attentive to how I felt around his family, Brad said he was going to say goodbye to his grandfather and we would leave. He wasn't there long at all and we headed out the same door as we had come in.

It seemed as though no one even knew we were gone, which didn't surprise me although it should have. I was just so glad that they live to on the West Coast and we live on the East Coast. Brad had one sister living in Texas one sister living in Arizona and a brother living in Nevada, at the time. Of course, we had our property in Florida which put us nearly 3000 miles apart from his family, thank God.

As we drove in silence, both of us lost in our thoughts, I wondered to myself if we could have done something differently to change the outcome of that evening. The timing wasn't right nor was there enough of it to strengthen our position.

We would be leaving their within the week. So we resigned ourselves to them dealing with their own feelings in their own time and concentrated on getting our business and relationship on a strong path. I knew that we would not have to deal with them face-to-face because of the distance between us for a long time to come.

This was a relief to me but possibly not to Brad. As I was an only child I was a bit selfish and not understanding of sibling relationships. Even to this day I don't understand them. Aren't we are all a work in progress?

Chapter Ten
Public Opinion

The next big hurdle that we would have to overcome would be the public's opinion of our relationship.

We had spoken of this briefly but had not yet encountered the full brunt of it. We had made a promise to one another that we would sometimes have to play the role of husband-and-wife and other times the role of mother and son, depending on the situation. A lot of my readers may not agree with me on this, however, I've been there and I understand the embarrassment and feelings of humiliation that are associated with people's misunderstandings.

For example; if we were to go to a restaurant and upon entering the establishment the maitre d' asked Brad would you and your mother like a table or booth, we would naturally play the mother and son role. Then on the other hand sometimes Brad would just say, "my wife and I would like a table for two".

Until one time Brad asked for a table for us, as husband and wife, and by the time we got sat down we were getting a lot of stares. We noticed the waiters and waitresses snickering at our expense. I overheard one older couple saying, what could they possibly have in common? We did not enjoy our meal at all and reserved ourselves to the fact that other people can't handle our relationship like we can.

After we left the restaurant and came home we sat and talked about the incident for a while. I shared with Brad that I was not ashamed of our age difference and he concurred. We came to the conclusion that it was other people's insecurities not our own. The conversation that we had that night has been a relief for me ever since. I'm sure that some of you will say to yourselves, I knew that would happen. Yes, you're right. We suspected that it would happen as well. However, when you live it and feel it and experience it first-hand its much, much different. It has a way of changing your mind and showing you different aspects of how people react to certain situations. You live and learn.

If we didn't have to go into detail with a given situation and they assumed we were mother and son, we played that role. If they thought we were business partners we concurred and played that role.

We could have gone against public opinion in every situation however, as much as we enjoy dining out, we decided that life is too short to argue with staring people and continue to have to explain ourselves because of their insecurities.

When we went to a doctor's office they naturally thought we were mother and son so we let it go at that and were able to enjoy ourselves. They were all strangers anyway and we would probably never see them again.

We were going to enjoy life and not worry about what the public opinion may be of our relationship.

It doesn't really matter whether it was right or wrong it's our life and we'll live it the way we see fit. Not conforming to what other people think that we should be.

Now I will say that all the festival people that we dealt with never did stare and approved of our relationship more than the public did.

You see in artists circles there are so many unusual couples and relationships that ours did not stand out. You have multiracial couples (black and white), couples with Down's syndrome children, etc. In the festival atmosphere they are not ostracized like they would be in public.

55

There are a lot of oddities in the arts world such as large, obese people with skinny people and of course, older women with younger men. Therefore we fit in, in their world and did not feel like outcasts.

If you have a hide like a rhinoceros you would be able to deal with the insults, the snickering and the stares. Fortunately, neither Brad nor I have rhinoceros hide.

Therefore, we decided to deal with the public's opinion or inadequacies as it were, in our own way.

We began to see that we were in for a totally different lifestyle than any relationship either one of us had ever been in. We had a special kinship at this point in our relation, thereby allowing us to work together on the subject of public opinion.

We've grown a lot since then. We still have an incident from time to time, but nothing like it used to be in the beginning.

We still create quite a stir in an atmosphere where they know we are husband and wife. It's almost comical to watch people's reaction. We just have fun with it now here it isn't that what life is supposed to be, fun?

Chapter Eleven
Friends' Indifference

Most of my girlfriends had been married for over 30 years and were very reserved in their approach to families. I had always been shy and dreaded telling my girlfriends what was happening in my personal life. All I had to do was tell one of them and they would all know. You know how women chit-chat. I was a private person and I really did not want them all to know about my personal business.

The calls started coming in from all the different girlfriends. And I said to myself get used to it Maureen, you either want to be in Brad's life or you can have all of these girls friendships, which will it be? What a joke their friendships turned out to be! The answer was, it's your life tell them the way it is.

It was a monumental task for me, I handled it. The friends I lost weren't friends in the first place. Although I thought they were. I found out later they weren't

Because my late husband traveled a great deal, he was not home very much. So I was always the one they called to do them a favor and go here and there with them for company, these so-called friends of mine.

After I met Brad, my time was being taken up with him and our relationship and boy were they angry. They certainly didn't like it or agree with it. I no longer had extra time to run here and there with them and it began to take its toll on our so-called friendships.

I decided for the first time in my life I would do my own thing on my own time and please myself for a change. They couldn't imagine me being with a man 29 years younger than myself. A lot of their comments were the same as the ones we got from the public opinion in restaurants, doctors offices, etc. What could they possibly have in common? Little did they know, we had more in common in the short time our relationship had existed, than they did with their husbands after 30 years of being married.

Slowly but ever so certainly the phone calls began to dwindle and eventually came to a halt. I was no longer there yes friend. I had changed from a people pleaser into someone who was now looking to please herself. If my memory serves me correctly it was less than a year before all of the phone calls completely stopped.

Even now, as we just celebrated our eighth wedding anniversary, they still contend that it will never last. We still hear from time to time the same old line, what could they possibly have in common?

I decided a long time ago to just let it go, forgive them for their nasty remarks, and accept that they will never change their minds about our age difference because they don't understand it. I doubt that they ever will. It's not an age thing with Brad and I, it's a heart thing. Our souls met, our hearts touched, and we've loved one another ever since. It's not a hard thing to understand. It's quite simple, it's love!

I've made a lot of new acquaintances. I call them "hello and goodbye friends". I tell them right away about our circumstances and if they don't agree or if they start acting funny, than we see less and less of them immediately. Eventually, it fades away. We may still see them occasionally but the friendship never deepens.

It's a backward standard that we have in this country. I mean, it's funny how a man perhaps 70 or 80 years old can take on a girlfriend who is 20 or 30 years old and that's OK! Society doesn't ask what they could possibly have in common, it says, isn't he's doing great to have such a young woman by his side?

However, reverse the roles with an older woman and a younger man and now she's a cradle robber or what they refer to as a 'cougar'.

Occasionally a bit of bitterness tends to come to the surface in my heart but it's getting less and less as time rolls on. You can't change the whole world or others perceptions of it. What you can do is live your own life and not worry about their ideals and perceptions. You have to change yourself and your own opinion of yourself and then live your own life.

There-in lies the reason that our relationship works, we don't allow outside influences or perceptions to shape our relationship. My advice to you older women would be to do the same. Love that younger man like you would if you had an older man, and don't let outside forces influence your relation with your man.

Until it happens to you, you feel the same way everyone else in the world does. I know in my heart it has given me a different perspective in life, being with a younger person. I've become much more compassionate and understanding to mixed couples, to interracial couples, and to the oddities of the world.

Sometimes I almost feel like going over to the people who snicker and stare and say, how would you feel if they were staring and snickering at you? Didn't your parents raise you with any decency or manners? Why don't you leave them alone and go about your own business? Grow up!

We have some friends who have a Down's syndrome son and he has really taken to us. He doesn't see our age difference. He sees our friendship. We've taken him out periodically for dinner and it's so painful to see others gawk at him. And to think that the parents allow it to happen is the real tragedy. We've even had parents who've allowed their youngsters to come over and ask what was wrong with our friend. What is wrong with the world today? Aren't we teaching our youngsters any manners or ethics or morals?

I have a special thing to say in those situations. It goes like this, God made him a little different than you and I, but he gave him a loving heart so he could be kind to others as we all should.

Chapter Twelve
Getting to Know One Another

There's an old saying that says "you don't know a person until you've lived with them". How true it is!

I learned that Brad was into spy and war movies. Now, there's nothing wrong with them I just have never enjoyed them. I like romantic movies, arts and entertainment channel, and current events. He's not so much into the romantic movies but he does like the current events. So, you see, I really didn't know him until we began to live together.

We both love to cook so that was a big plus. We also both enjoy going to antique markets, museums, and seminars together.

It's really hard to get to know each other fully without living with that person. I know the conservative mindset says that you should not live together until you're married. I feel that it's a New World however, and we learn by doing.

I know that as we dated when we were younger we all put on our acts. But when you live your day-to-day life with someone you become much more aware of the differences and similarities. At which time you can tend to them or ignore them.

Brad and I have chosen to discuss them as they come up. We tend to them immediately and then go on with our life. This makes our relationship much closer and stronger. I recommend this highly to the older women who choose to be with a younger man. For that matter, I would recommend it to any couple. Honesty is definitely the best policy and discussing and dealing with these situations as they come up is most important to a successful marriage. It works for us. I know it will work for you.

As we began to get to know one another I found that through our many ups and downs I'd rather jot down a note or send a card or letter to speak my heart. And, me being a writer, it was something I enjoyed anyway. So we would send love notes back and forth to one another. Even to this day he still buys me cards and brings me flowers. Sometimes writing your feelings is better than speaking them. Not always, sometimes though!

It didn't surprise me when I was so overwhelmed with love for Brad that I'd write him a love note instead of telling him. That fits the pattern of Maureen. I personally found it much more romantic to put it in writing. Besides getting love notes at my age makes me feel young again.

I would write a love note put some of my favorite perfume on it and put it in a place that he often went where I knew he'd find it. He would get the note, answer it, and send one back my way. Not immediately though, as he knew I anticipated its arrival. When I least expected I'd find a note. Often times in places I didn't expect to find them. I'd be taking a nap and a crumpled note would fall out of the pillow slip, or I'd clean the table and I'd find a note under my plate. It truly is a match made in heaven.

Brad and I still write notes to one another after eight years. In a strange sort of way this book is like a love note between Brad and I. I am learning more about him and vice-versa.

As we traveled around the different festivals the whole world began to take on a different meaning for me. Brad was beginning to bring out the young woman in me.

We began to take our breaks together and eventually it led to, where are you going next week? I knew exactly where I'd be going, but I didn't want to let on to him, so I would act naive and say oh, I'm not sure! He would say to me well then let's go together.

He had already helped me make some changes in my booth that were very important and it really helped my sales. I needed him more than I was willing to admit. And of course, I couldn't let him know it. Not yet anyway! I would say to him that's a good idea, let's combine the gross and split the expenses.

He is so handy when it comes to mechanics and design and a lot of other things. I thought to myself this could be a very profitable venture, not to mention the rest of the relationship.

Each night after work we would drive and find an all-night diner. Sometimes it was miles and miles from anywhere, which gave us time to talk. He was uniquely different than anyone I'd ever met. We acted like teenagers sometimes. However, we were not acting, this was reality.

It was so nice to have him to check the tires, check the oil, and do all of the man things to my vehicles. I was brought up a lady, doing lady like things. Vehicles are not a girls place. We would make the trip's convoy style until we arrived at our next festival. He and I would then go choose a motel. I recall the very first motel lobby, when I said, let's get to know one another better.

Our next festival would be Niagara Falls New York. Niagara Falls is such a romantic place. The falls themselves made it all worthwhile.

Chapter Thirteen
Marriage and Honeymoon

Our season was over and vacation time was ahead of us. Brad had already received a phone call from a company that wanted him to come to work for them as soon as we got back to Tampa. It would be four months before we would be back out on the road again and we had to fill the void financially.

We had already decided that we would be married that winter. Not having a lot of time to prepare or send out invitations, we decided to we would go to the courthouse downtown Tampa, Florida and be married by the justice of the peace. Our two closest friends agreed to stand up for us at our wedding. We had gone three days prior to get the marriage license and necessary documents in order.

I decided to go shopping. I purchased a beige chiffon wedding dress with shoes and a purse to match. Brad bought me two dozen red roses to top it all off. I carried several red roses with me during the wedding ceremony.

The gentleman and lady who conducted our ceremony at the courthouse were so kind to us. It made us feel very comfortable and at ease. After the formalities of the ceremony inside the courthouse, we took all the pictures outside.

After we were done our friends took us to a restaurant called the Southern Tea Room. It was decorated with Victorian furnishings like something out of the 1800's. Even the hostess and wait staff were dressed in old Victorian outfits. The women had on long, floor length dresses with fancy little aprons, and the small decorated hat on their head. Me being an old-fashioned girl, I felt right at home.

There was a gift shop in the lobby of the restaurant filled with old-time knick-knacks and memorabilia. Brad bought me an antique oil lamp as I have a collection of them. We planned to come back there many times in the future.

After we had a wonderful time at the restaurant, our friends dropped us off at the house. A couple of hours later they arrived back at our house with a wedding gift for us. My friend had gone and had our wedding pictures developed and put into a large silver frame with beautiful antique etching around it. I would treasure it for years to come.

That night Brad took me to an Oceanside hotel. We so enjoyed each other's company that evening. That is a night that I will always cherish deeply. Our first time together, intimately, was wonderful. However, our wedding night together was indescribable. He was such a gentleman and I felt like such a lady. He made me feel young again and again and again.

The next morning I got the surprise of my life. We drove back to our house and Brad told me we need to pack a suitcase for at least a week. He told me he was taking me to New Orleans, Louisiana for our honeymoon. He knew that it was my favorite place to be. He had planned a big trip for us for months. I was so excited. I felt like a little girl again. We packed our bags and away we went. It would be a six or 700 mile trip, but being so used to traveling all the time it was nothing for us.

We arrived in Louisiana about midday the following afternoon. After checking into a French Quarter Inn we stepped out onto the balcony to look at the city. It truly is a breathtaking sight.

The French quarter has an old-time feel to it. Most of that area was built in the 16th and 17th centuries. It is filled with historical monuments, landmarks and buildings.

After we settled into our room, we went downstairs and began walking till we found an elegant dining establishment on Bourbon Street. There was a beautiful cathedral on the way, at Jackson Square, so we stopped and took a look. On the left-hand side of Jackson Square was an old-time apartment building. We asked a local the name of the building. He replied, that's the Pontalba apartment building. It's the oldest in the United States, said the local resident. I've always felt connected to the New Orleans area. It's as if I've lived there before, if you know what I mean.

We found our way to the restaurant and began to read the menu board that was out on the sidewalk. If you've ever been to New Orleans you know that all of the restaurants, or most of them anyway, have menu boards out on the sidewalks.

I remember my meal distinctly. I had a peppercorn, dry rubbed sirloin steak covered with burgundy wine sauce that was out of this world, real garlic mashed potatoes, corn on the Cobb and a couple of hot tea. It's no wonder that people rave about that restaurant. It was one of the best meals I've ever had in my life. I was so full that I just have a couple of bites of Brad's desert, which was baked Alaska.

After we ate we wander around the French quarter for several more hours. It really comes alive at night so there was plenty to see. I haven't had that much fun since I was a child going to the movies back home. I always feel so at home in New Orleans. It was a breathtaking experience and one I won't soon forget.

The atmosphere in New Orleans is such that it brings people closer together at heart. Brad brought me flowers several times that week. He would have breakfast delivered to our room so that we didn't have to go out early. We visited the sites around New Orleans at our leisure, and promised ourselves we would spend as many anniversaries there in New Orleans as we could.

As the week began to draw to a close Brad took me to several collectibles shops and bought us some memorabilia, including a can of French pralines.

Our week ended all too soon. Neither of us wanted to leave. I wished, at that point, that it could be that way forever. As we looked over the city our last evening there, we realized how in love we both were with one another and the French quarter. It had been unforgettable week for both of us. I fell asleep to sweet dreams.

The next morning we had our final breakfast in New Orleans. We packed up all our belongings and put everything in the vehicle.

We set out towards Tampa and followed the coastline as much as we could. This really is a beautiful country that we live in.

We took our time going back. We stopped that night on the Alabama coast near Mobile. What a beautiful area that is by the Gulf coast.

The next day we drove on into Tampa. Brad called the company where he would be working for the winter. They had wanted him to come to work the previous week so they were ecstatic to hear that he was back in town. Our winter went smooth and before we know it we were back out on the road again traveling to our first festival.

Chapter Fourteen
Married Life with 29 Years Difference

I had begun to see the fullness of getting to know someone by living with them. Now that we were married it became more and more prevalent.

Something as simple as knowing how he likes his coffee and eggs in the morning made it so much easier to understand one another. Because we both enjoy cooking, that particular aspect came more natural to us than did others.

Things such as appearance were where we clashed most often. Coming from different eras he was much more concerned with appearance than I was. Take for instance going to the grocery store, before I would just throw on an old pair of pants and an old shirt and would be ready to go. No makeup, simple shoes, more for comfort than for looks. I now felt that I wanted to dress up more than before. So I would find a nice blouse and take more time with my makeup, putting on perfume and jewelry for appearance sake.

So my appearance became a much larger aspect of my life now that I was with a younger man. For example, before, I had worn the typical granny gowns for years. Now I found myself buying negligees and the like. I eventually got rid of all of my old style granny gowns, ha, ha, ha. My whole reason for living had changed.

All the way down to my footwear, I began to get rid of the old and bring in the new. I began to develop a more modern style for my appearance. I bought myself a pair of high-heeled, thigh-high boots, new sexier underwear, tighter shirts and pants, etc., etc. I never realized before now, how much your clothes create an atmosphere of youth within and without oneself. They can make you look younger and feel younger, too.

When my late husband and I would go shopping, I got used to staying in the vehicle while he went in the stores. With the exception of grocery shopping I generally stayed in the car. Now that I was with Brad, I wouldn't stay in the vehicle at all. I would jump out immediately and go with him, even into the hardware stores which don't interest me at all.

We have developed a habit of walking in the evenings, whereas before I hardly walked at all with my previous husband.

Not only am I learning a lot about life, but also a lot about myself in the process. You're only as young as you feel. As I began to surround myself with younger circumstances and situations, being with a younger man, I began to feel younger myself not only outwardly, but in my soul as well.

With my first husband there were very few outings or activities. However, now that I am with Brad we have begun to explore many, many avenues that I had always wanted to explore.

He takes me to concerts, to the park, or just for a ride around the town at Christmastime to look at the lights. I have begun to feel young at heart once again.

And this is what I want to convey to my readers, especially my older, female readers. You don't have to wait to feel young again. It can happen in the blink of an eye. You too, can actively seek out a younger mate and get on with your life.

Too many of my older friends with families sit at home all alone waiting for an occasion to arise so they can have the company of family. Birthdays, weddings, holidays and so on.

Their family members never encourage them to seek out a companion. It's sad to think that their families would rather see them alone and unhappy than to be with someone that fulfills them and brings them joy.

Many of my friends tell me how lucky I am to have a younger man in my life. They tell me I seem more vibrant, more alive, and that I even appear younger than I used to. I attribute this to my relationship with Brad, 29 years difference and all.

Every day I experience differences in our lives. Coming from different eras makes it a challenge on a daily basis. I was raised in a much different environment than he was. As our differences arise we meet them head-on. We throw them out on the table, discuss them, come up with solutions, and get on with our lives.

The longer we're together the more in tune we become with one another's idiosyncrasies. They not only create a challenge for us, they make us stronger by bringing us closer to one another through discussions and problem-solving. Teamwork if you will.

My main goal for writing this book is to provide hope where there is none. To create a helpful situation where there's helplessness. To show the world, through the example of my life, that age truly has a bearing on a relationship, but it should not define the relationship.

You too, can have a wonderful existence living with a younger man. There is truly someone for everyone. I am only one in a myriad of examples of how age-gap relationships can be rewarding and fulfilling.

All relationships require hard work, trust, loyalty, honesty and commitment. Age gap relationships are no different, but in my humble opinion they are more rewarding and fulfilling.

He brings me youth and I bring him wisdom. He brings me vigor and I bring him stability. He brings me excitement and I bring him experience. We bring one another happiness and true love. What more could one ask for from life?

Chapter Fifteen
Health Problems

I had always been blessed with good health in my younger years. The only childhood disease that I had was measles. All the other kids, at different times, would be home with one childhood disease or another. I don't ever remember getting all of those childhood diseases, like they had. I was kept in a dark bedroom when I had the measles. I'm sure they don't do that today.

Up to my 50s I was comparatively healthy. Until one day when I was walking with my friends. There was a small incline ahead of us and all of the sudden I said I can't make it up that hill. They all asked me what was wrong, and of course I said I don't know. I was not out of breath, but I had a foreboding fear that something bad would happen if I continued to walk up that hill. A woman's intuition, if you will. We turned around and went back to our respective homes. The next morning I called my late husband's cardiologist, who told me to come in immediately for a checkup.

After my examination he immediately told me that he was going to put me in touch with a surgeon who would perform a catheterization. After he performed many tests I was informed that I had four blockages in my heart. I would be admitted immediately for heart surgery. The next morning they operated. I had quadruple bypass surgery.

I don't recall being in any pain at all. The worst part of the entire operation, for me, was the tube down the throat. It was a choking, awful feeling. Anyone having gone through that surgery knows what I'm talking about.

My stay in the hospital was extremely short for that type of surgery. I was only there four days. Up to that point in my life I had been quite healthy. The diabetes that had been diagnosed in 1980 had led to my heart surgery in 1995. Looking back I wish I had done things differently concerning my diet. I may never have had to have bypass surgery. But, all in all, I am quite healthy even through all of this.

My recuperation period was short as well. I am very strong physically and emotionally. Both of these have got me through a lot of adversity in my life.

The diabetes also created some other harmful conditions in my health, the main one being my eye problem, macular degeneration. This is very common to diabetics. Diabetes does not generally create complete blindness. However, it does bring about a condition known as legal blindness.

I have endured several laser surgeries to both eyes to correct the bleeding that occurs in the macula from the diabetic condition. The laser surgery stops the vessels the eye from continuing to rupture. This in turn slows down the progression of the degeneration. It is only for a time, unfortunately. We continually search for new alternatives to this ever-increasing problem. They have some cutting edge technologies coming out now that may help in the future.

Other then these two conditions I have the normal age-related problems. Such as arthritis, joint stiffness, etc.

Just recently there was one new development. In April of 2006 Brad took me to the hospital because I couldn't keep any food down. Neither of us expected it to be serious, although it turned out to be.

After running their battery of tests on me the Dr. concluded that I was having a mild heart attack. Once again there was no pain due to the fact that the diabetes kills the nerve endings in its subject.

They rushed me up to the cardio wing of the hospital and once again I had a catheterization. They concluded that there was a blockage in the carotid artery and that a stent would be necessary. Thank the good Lord for today's technology. They now have a stent that releases a drug around the area so that the cartilage does not build up as it did with the old ones. After they operated on me and installed the stent, the doctor informed me I did not have a heart attack in the first place.

Nonetheless, thank God we went when we did. I was only there for two days this time. Once again I attributed it to my strength of mind and having a younger man in my life. He gave me strength, encouragement and he never left my side. It was wonderful to have the love of an individual, regardless of his age, that would love me in sickness and in health as were our vows when we got married. His youth and vigor put me on the road to recovery right away.

As I look back now I compare my late husband being gone most of the time after my first surgery to Brad being by my side constantly after my second surgery. There's no comparison. Having a younger man couldn't be more fulfilling for me. I would encourage any older woman, tired of not having a companion, to seek out the youth of today. Through vigilance and prayer God will bring you the mate of your dreams.

There is hope for us, the older generation, through the youth of our world. Seek and ye shall find, Knock and it shall be opened unto you, Ask you shall receive. Words to live by!

Chapter Sixteen
Things in Common

In all relationships you often hear "what could they possibly have in common?" but especially in an Age Gap Relationships. In our relationship we have discovered that we have much more in common than we ever thought in the beginning.

Let's begin with loving to fly. Brad and I both adore it. The more we travel this way the more excitement we have towards this type of travel. I never was much for flying before I met Brad, possibly because I would be doing it alone. My first husband wasn't much of a couples oriented type person. He was more of one to do things on his own. Once Brad and I got together I found a lot of things that I had never enjoyed before became enjoyable because I had someone to do them with.

One thing that I found out immediately was that Brad likes the Blues. He enjoys Blues music, old Ragtime, Dixieland and he is a lover of New Orleans, as am I.

We both enjoy music in the morning. Sometimes we play blues sometimes its country and other times its jazz. I feel like it's the variety as well as enjoying the same types of music that has drawn us closer together over the years.

We also both enjoy meditative music. Occasionally we'll listen to some old classic rock 'n' roll, or some classical. The diversity of our likes and dislikes has brought a wonderful aspect to the table in our relationship. I had never experienced it at this level before.

Another thing that Brad and I have in common is our love of food and preparing it. He was raised in a family that was very food oriented. With seven children you can see why. His mother cooked from scratch on a consistent basis, as did mine.

His mother and father owned and ran a restaurant for part of his childhood. Naturally, he helped them run it because he enjoyed the food business as well. Never having been a big seafood fan myself I learned to enjoy many, many types of seafood dishes that Brad would prepare for us.

He taught me how to cook rainbow trout that is out of this world. He has a recipe for shrimp scampi that'll make your mouth water just to smell it. Over the years we have invented many new different types of seafood plates that we both enjoy thoroughly.

Another one of our common denominators is our love of movies. He's not real big on the love stories, as most men aren't. However, he will sit through them with me. We both enjoy westerns, dramas, medical investigations, mysteries, documentaries, and anything concerning animals. That brings me to my next point.

I have always loved animals since I was a child. Come to find out so has Brad. I am more of a cat lover and he is more into dogs. However, being out on the road traveling with our business, we didn't have dogs. Cats are much more easily taken care of than dogs. Dogs require space to run plus being let outside and walked all the time. With a dog you can't leave them alone for more than a few hours at a time. You might be able to leave them for an eight hour day, but you wouldn't be able to leave them for a couple of days.

It's different with cats. You can put down extra food and water then go away for the weekend. They are much more self-reliant and self-sufficient. Not to say that we don't love dogs because we do, just to say that cats are more readily taken care of on the road.

All of that was about to change, although, at the time, we didn't know it. In the last couple of years since we've stopped traveling for a living, we have wanted to get a small dog. Lo and behold our wishes came true one sunny afternoon. We were coming down the freeway near Tampa and got off on an exit that we very rarely take. As we rounded the exit Brad saw a little bobbing head jumping through the tall grass. He got excited as he pulled off the exit on the wrong side of the road. He ran through the tall grass and scooped up what would be the biggest bundle of joy that had come into our lives in a long time. It was a Terrier, Chihuahua mix puppy. He was sent from heaven like a little angel, so we called him Spirit. He was sent to us just at the right time, also.

Brad began to work locally and was gone for at least eight hours a day. Of course I was at home alone. Our little dog has brought me so much companionship and love that it is unbelievable. What a precious gift he has been to both of us.

Of course we still have our four cats, two of which stay outside and two of which are inside cats. So our love of animals has brought us closer together.

Naturally, we both enjoy writing therefore it has been a love affair collaborating on this book. Brad has had some of his poetry published in the past. I feel that this book is bringing us closer together as we write it. We are learning more and more about one another as the weeks roll on. It has brought to light a lot of our likes and dislikes. There are very few things that we don't have in common.

Traveling is another one of our in common loves. We met out on the road which is one dead giveaway. We kept our traveling business together for almost 7 years.

Our hope is that this book will touch others' lives and bring them the joy and happiness that we have sought and found in one another. Our love of traveling will be renewed through promoting this book out on the road.

Interior decorating combines our love of country settings and our love of antiques. Our quaint little home in Florida is a perfect example of the two coming together. It is filled with antiques, memorabilia from past years, and country style decorations. It has a pot belly stove right in the kitchen. We use it for heat in the winter which is fairly short in Florida.

Brad was raised in a country environment and so was I. Therefore our love of country surroundings is definitely something we share.

Brad and I have found that because we have so much in common it has made it easier for us to get along with one another. When your mate enjoys doing the same things you do it makes it so much easier to pick places to go and things to do.

The one thing that I would say to the older women who are reading this book is to search out that younger person you can see has the same things in common that you enjoy in life. Search for the qualities in a person that you admire. It takes time but it is well worth the wait.

Ever since I got older I've associated more with younger people. I understand them better and get along with them better, due to their flexibility. As I got to know Brad I found out that he has associated with older people most of his life. He told me he's always had more in common with older people.

It seems like every day we find more things that we have in common. It's such a joy to be able to do things with a companion by your side. What a gift it is to truly connect with another soul.

It's easy for me to understand how we get along so well. For years and years before I met Brad I knew intuitively there would be a man from the West Coast who I would meet and my longings for a soul-mate would end. Colorado was uppermost in my mind, and had been for years.

When I found out that Brad was from Colorado I knew he was the one. The longing for my soul-mate has gone now. This proves to me that he is the one. The longing subsided and our love began.

I hope and pray that the older women out there will begin their search for a soul-mate. Whether he's a little younger or much younger makes no difference. Age difference is a faux pas of society. Going against the grain can be wonderfully exciting and fulfilling. Other people's ideas and thoughts on this subject are exactly that, their ideas.

You must decide for yourself who on this earth makes you happy and fulfills your desire to be with a soul-mate. It is true there is someone for everyone.

I thank the heavens above that this young man was brought into my life. Don't ever give up. Keep searching. He's out there waiting for you to find him.

Chapter Seventeen
My Advice to Older Women

First of all you must decide if you want a younger man. This may take you days or months to make up your mind but either way it's very important. The length of time it takes you to decide will tell you what your decision should be. If it takes you too long to make up your mind than your heart has made up your mind for you, it's a big NO. The decision must ultimately be yours. It's not an easy conclusion to come to and it's a lifelong choice. So be wise and follow your heart.

I'd like to address the ladies with families. Your choice will ultimately be much harder than those ladies without them.

You will have to deal with criticisms, comments generally being negative, and advice based on their perception of how you should live your life.

Once again, the decision is ultimately yours not theirs. Others perception's of how you should live will most assuredly be the opposite of how you truly want to live. Your well-being and happiness is at stake here, not theirs. Although they want you to be happy, they're not the ones that will be living in the situation, you will.

Your ultimate goal should be to find the person that makes you the happiest. For me that was a younger man. I have found contentment, joy and peace beyond what I could've imagined. I wish that for you as well.

I'll move on to the widow who doesn't have family or their families don't live nearby. This is the case with me. My daughter is thousands of miles away and I don't have any other family members living besides her. My daughter has been very supportive of me, because she has my best interest at heart. I'm sure she has questions in the back of her mind, but she doesn't let that interfere with our relationship. In fact, she is helping me edit this book. She senses that I am happy inside and therefore she supports me. I am lucky in that respect.

So the widow sits at home alone. She'll go shopping a couple times a week alone. She goes to church alone. She eats alone, watches TV alone, reads alone, and goes to bed alone. How truly sad that is.

For some reason she doesn't want to go against her family by getting together with a younger man. I have several lady friends in this situation.

When you've made up your mind that you're going to begin looking for a younger man, this is the foundation for you to build from, honesty, trust, and a sense of calm about his spirit. Don't do it based on the negativity from friends and family, rather do it for your own companionship based on your own close observations of him.

Now to begin building the house, don't be hesitant to go to places where younger men congregate. Outdoor sports are always the right choice. Art festivals are also a great decision. It's a wonderful place to find a variety of age groups. Broadway shows, especially at intermission are a perfect venue for older women searching for that younger man. One could also join a volunteer charity Association which is also a good way to meet people of all ages.

Now some of you might happen to have families who are negative towards you dating. It is best if you see the person for a while before you upset your family with the good news. This way if it doesn't work out between you two there's no upset. Most of your friends will question you many times over and some will disappear because they disagree with you so much. If you are strong you will say, "for once in my life I'm going to please me".

I think we'll all agree that 15% of married couples are still together because of the family, kids, bills, etc. However when one of the spouses passes away you feel liberated somehow and truly feel" free at last".

One of your happiest days will be when a relative approves of your choice of relationships.

If your family is up north and you're in the South or vice versa, again it makes it easier. You can avoid a telephone call but when you live in the same city, town or area it is very hard to fib to a loved one. It might feel like you're being a little underhanded, but you're actually sparing them a lot of worry and agony.

A lot of single men go to the zoo. They may take nieces and nephews or stepchildren with them. This would be a good place to find a variety of ages. It's easy to figure out if he is the father. Talking about the animals will really help to start a conversation. And so here we have a few places you could go in order to mingle with the proper age group.

Now, mind you, there will be women who just cannot relate, and that's OK. Not everyone can imagine life with a younger man. And that's OK. I've always thought of a relationship or marriage as cultivating a garden. You plant the bulbs and the seeds. You fertilize them, water them, nurture them, and then you choose your most favorite for a bouquet or a single rose.

All the work of the garden becomes a labor of love. All the hours of picking the weeds, cutting, edge trimming, and when a plant dies you feel terrible. Because it was a part of you, you say to yourself, I wonder what I could've done to save that precious part of this plant. Sometimes you feel that it was your fault but we all know that all things pass away in time.

So it is with searching for younger men. You must tend to it daily like a garden by giving it care and tenderness. Eventually it will sprout the beautiful flowers of a relationship.

Chapter Eighteen
Friends First Then Lovers

In today's society if you can say your husband is your best friend you are well on your way to wedded bliss, as they say.

Brad and I are able to talk over many things as they come up. That makes it so much easier when a mountain appears. Don't get me wrong we've had plenty of our own mountains to climb but with patience and prayer we've been able to surmount all obstacles.

I have so many friends that say they are not friends with their husbands or wives but rather they're merely a sexual habit instead. This to me is so sad. I feel very badly when I hear these things. They can't sit down and have a quiet conversation especially about money without having a debate. They say if you can count on one hand your friends, you are most fortunate. How true that is in today's society.

I count on Brad as my best friend daily. He's always there and he always will be. In another month it will be eight years since we got married and we are still on our honeymoon.

We were best friends first then lovers and what a difference it has made in our relationship.

Candlelit dinners and slow walks on the beach at sunset, these are a few of my favorite things, how about you? It doesn't have to be a romantic scene it just has to be. Once you've met him get to know him. Become his friend. Show him what true friendship is all about. You'll be amazed what you'll get in return.

To really know your mate doesn't happen until you live with them, but spending weekends together can make all the difference. This does not have to mean sexually because there are many ways to become intimate without performing the actual acts.

Nothing new can come into your life unless you are grateful. When you become more aware you become more grateful. Think, believe and receive. Your destiny awaits you.

Chapter Nineteen
Letters from All Over

(May \ Dec) Relationships: Looking for letters from other couples and interested singles.

Your letters and E-mails will help so many people in their quest for happiness. Our E-mail address is: (brama813@yahoo.com). Please send us your stories and experiences. We will e-mail the necessary forms of affidavit for all written entries.

There are many new words associated with our type of book. One of those is "Cougar", meaning, a woman of middle age who actively seeks the casual companionship of younger (typically under thirty years of age) males.

Another catch phrase would be "Kitten". This one has its origins from the mass media. Several cases across the U.S.A. have involved a woman in her early 20's and a younger male in his mid to late teens. A kitten is described as a young woman typically 18-23 years of age who seeks a much younger male usually mid to late teens for a permanent companion.

As I sat and thought about those terms I began to form one of my own, in my mind. I thought to myself I was 61 when our relationship began and have always considered myself a conservative, mature, educated lady who wouldn't think of going to a bar or a dance club to meet younger men.

A word came into my mind as I sat and thought about our relationship. That word was, "Lioness". The lioness does most of the hunting for the family. She is the older, more dominant female. She is strong, intelligent, cunning, and a playful companion. As I thought about the lioness I felt a bond with her. Yes, I am a lioness.

Like the lioness I was seeking the companionship of a younger stronger, dominant male.

BRAD'S VIEWPOINT

Chapter One
Growing Up

I was born a beautiful spring day, in March of 1965. It was the 30th day of March. My mother said she had less labor with me than with my other three siblings. It was 8:02 a.m., and I came into this world in the usual way. No special ceremonies, no banners waving, just the usual birth. I was 9 lbs. 8 oz., which is big for any baby.

I can remember my mother telling me later on in life, that she had told my brothers and sisters to be nice to me, because I was going to end up being bigger than all of them. Of course mothers have that intuition and she was right, I am.

It was still cold in Denver that day, as I came into this world. Of course I don't remember it, although sometimes I wish I did.

I don't remember the first house that we lived in when I was born. I've been told about it by my brothers and sisters. The first house I remember was our second house. It was on Lyden Street, close to Washington Avenue. We lived about five blocks from Washington high school where we used to go to swim in the pool.

For the first five or six years of my life, we had the typical, normal family life.

I remember the winters as the snow plows would pile snow as high as me on the sides of the road. I can remember seeing snow banks five or 6 feet tall, of course taller than me. How vivid some memories are and then others seem to fade with time.

I remember specific things about the house, the yard, the garage, the street, and the surrounding houses. And yet I couldn't tell you what

I had for dinner 2 weeks ago. The strange things in life are what make life special.

I remember things like my father bringing home a derby car, and letting me and my older brothers and sisters smash it to pieces with sledgehammers. Of course there was one stipulation, no breaking the glass. It was an understood thing about not getting glass all over the driveway. So my brother and I took those sledgehammers and pounded in every piece of metal on that car. Man did we have a blast. I remember it as if it was yesterday.

As I look back now it was a great way for us to take out our frustrations. It was like therapy. Of course, I didn't see it that way back then, however, I definitely see it that way now.

We had a trampoline in our backyard. I can remember the neighbors across the street from us coming over to the house, knocking on the door, and telling my mother they thought there was something funny going on in the backyard with the kids. They kept seeing our heads coming up above the house, and wondered if my father was being mean to us. Of course, I thought it was funny, but as I look back it wasn't funny at all, once again the strange things in life.

Much like that trampoline ride, my life had many ups and downs. I recall my father setting a bale of hay and some heavy cardboard inside our house, in front of the bay window that looked out at the backyard. He had bought a new compound bow and wanted to try it out, but it was too cold outside. So he set up his target inside the house.

His first shot at the target went through the hay, through the cardboard, and through the window, ending up in the backyard. These were the kind of antics that I grew up around.

My mother told me about a time when I was five or six years old when, in my Sunday best clothes, I climbed to the top of our oak tree. Naturally, I was trying to get attention, and it worked. However, it was not the type of attention I was looking for.

So there was little Brad in his little suit and tie, 20 feet up in a tree, smiling and having a good time. Out comes my mother screaming at me for messing around in my church clothes.

In actuality, I frightened her to death being so far up in a tree. I wasn't what you would call a little troublemaker, although sometimes I did get into a bit of mischief.

There was one other occasion, living on that street, when I decided I was going to run away from home. I distinctly remember my mother helping me pack a small suitcase. She asked me where I was going to work, what I was going to eat, and where I would go to live. Of course, at that age, I didn't have any answers for her questions.

So I took my little suitcase and I walked off down the street. The suitcase was half again my size. I went to an abandoned brick building that my brother and I used to play at about a block and a half from our house.

I stayed there for several hours crying, not knowing what I would do or where I would go. As I look back now, I feel that I was more hurt my mother had sent me away, then I was being on my own all alone. I would've been about eight years old at the time.

I actually didn't mind being alone, which is kind of strange for a small kid. I can remember by the time I was in my early teens I was attracted to women much older than myself, late teens or early 20s perhaps. Once again it seemed strange back then, but I would come to find out that it was just the way my character was designed.

I can remember trying to talk to the older girls, but they wouldn't have anything to do with me because I was just a little guy at the time. Once in awhile I would get one of them to pay attention to me and I would be in heaven for a little while. It would carry throughout my life, this desire for older women.

I must say though, that it was not a sexual desire like it is today. It was a desire to be around older more intelligent women. I would go through life enjoying older women's company more than the younger crowd.

89

Chapter Two
Early Adulthood

I went from the growing up years into my early teens with the same desire for older women. I distinctly remember in junior high being attracted to a couple of my teachers. There was one blonde teacher who taught seventh-grade English, and man was she a looker. Of course I was just a child at the time, although I thought I was a big man, like every man does in his teen years.

About halfway through the year of my seventh grade year, which would have been 1978, I met a 17 year-old senior from a different high school. We started dating and it lasted until my ninth-grade year. She and I ended up going to her prom dance together, which made me feel like a real big shot.

There I was 13 years old buying orchid corsages, boutineers, renting a tuxedo & limousine to go to the senior prom with an older woman. I suspect it had something to do with my size at that time in my life.

I have been over 6 feet tall since I was in the seventh-grade. I can remember walking down the hallways of my junior high and being a head taller than everyone else. There's just something about being with an older woman that always made me feel mature and much more secure.

So after the dance I can remember the feeling of wanting to get her home on time, to avoid getting in trouble, when in reality I was the one that needed to be home on time. Life has a funny way of throwing curve balls at you.

I felt I needed to rent the limousine because I wasn't even old enough to have a drivers license or vehicle to take her to the prom. Although I do recall learning to drive at a much younger age like 10 or 11 years old. And of course I have some crazy stories about learning to drive cars and how that all came about, but of course that's another story for another time.

About this time in my life my parents separated and got a divorce. It was about the worst time in my life that could've happened. At that age you look to your father figure for direction and answers to all life's questions. Well, I had no direction or answers because I had no father figure. My mother was a tremendous help but it's not the same. I needed a male figure to be a role model. So it is with much of our youth in today's society.

I was lucky in some respects. I was big enough to play football so I had a coach as a mentor. I remember having two or three different coaches because we moved around so much.

I recall going to three or four different high schools in the 4 years that make up high school. My grandfather was around some of the time as he was a minister at a local church. He wanted to be a mentor to us grandchildren but his schedule was too busy and took him away from us a lot.

I can remember my mother working all the time to support the four children after my father left. She was gone a lot which left us kids with extra time on our hands.

In some aspects it was cool to be a teenager with very little supervision. I suppose there were more disadvantages to it than advantages, as I look back. Such as having to cook for yourself or look after your own room and all your own stuff.

There was never a parent around to ask for a ride to the movie theater or to a friend's house. So you either had to ride your bike or walk. Although I do recall both my parents loving us four kids very much. I always felt loved.

My early teen years would find me working in restaurants to make spending money and to try and get enough saved up for a vehicle. There wasn't much monetarily with four kids and no father. So whatever we wanted we had to go get on our own, which, as I look back now, was one of the best lessons I could've learned at such an early age.

That lesson is, "Nothing in Life is Free." If you want something in life you must put out the energy to go get it. First, you have to see the goal. Next, you implement strategies to go and reach that goal. And thirdly, you get off your lazy duff and" just go do it".

I can recall working in restaurants until I was early to mid-20s. At which point I switched to the glass business. I would have been 22 at the time and I was looking toward starting a career.

Being a glass installer, once again put me in the situations where I would be around older women. First it was restaurants that it was the glass business. Both of which put me around older women all the time

Repairing broken windows and installing mirrors put me in houses with older women all the time. I can remember dating older women from the time I was in junior high till now. Some of them I met installing glass. Others I met through acquaintances or friends.

It would be a pattern that would stay with me for the rest of my life. And while they were all memorable experiences, there is one that stands out above all the others. That one would be my current wife Maureen. We'll get to that in a later chapter. For now, let's get back to my 20s. At the age of 21 I found out that my father had passed away. As you know he and my mother separated when I was 12. I never saw him again after that. It was a devastating blow to a 21 year-old hoping to have his questions answered by his father.

Questions like, why did you leave in the first place? What caused it? How could you leave us and never call again? Didn't you love us? A lot of things go through a 21 year-old mind in a crisis such as this.

Here I am 20 plus years later with only some of the answers to those questions concerning my father. My mother was a big help in relating to me my father's character. This was a tremendous help in sorting through all my grief and weird feelings.

I honestly believe that his character flaws are what caused him to make such bad decisions. Regardless, I moved on with my life and drew strength from the experience.

As I sit here remembering my 20s, I recall that my mother was several years older than my father. So it runs in the family.

If I remember correctly both of my older sisters have had several relationships with younger men in their lifetime.

I believe my brother is the only one that hasn't dated older women. He liked the younger girls. Not a problem, to each his own.

The older woman/younger man situation in relationships doesn't work for everybody. But to those that feel as I do, congratulations, you're in a special group of people like myself and my wife. My hope is that this book will give you some insight into the life of a younger man loving an older woman.

As I share my experiences with my readers, I want there to be a feeling of conduciveness. My wife and I want to share with the world how special our relationship is, not only to us but to those around us.

I feel that sharing my life experiences will help younger men when it comes to learning the when where why and how, in the world of dating older women.

You will gain insights of my knowledge and experiences. You will be able to draw from those your own conclusions and find your way towards a wonderful relationship with an older woman. It's not an easy path, but then again, nothing in life that is worth having comes easy.

A lot of times it seems that we want what we can't have or the road seems too rough to reach what we strive for. Sometimes both apply. So I searched my own soul to find definitive help for those in these situations.

This is a portion of what I came up with after thinking long and hard. The road to success and happiness is not easy for the simple fact that the trials and tribulations along the way are what shape and create the strength that you require to reach your goal. Once you learn that these bumps in the road are put there to better our character and to strengthen our resolve you become at peace with yourself and the world around you.

If the road was easy and void of strength and character building trials you would never appreciate actually realizing your goals and dreams because you wouldn't have enough strength of character to reach them.

It's like the spoiled rich kids whose silver spoon fed lives makes him weak unless they are made to support themselves, create a living for themselves, and create for themselves a future they are lonely souls full of depression.

I recall in my mid-20s reading an article about a scientific study that was conducted on children between the ages of 10 and 18. Half of the group was given strict discipline and rules to follow.

There were consequences for the wrong actions such as spanking, grounding, timeouts, and the like. This first group grew up with dignity, honesty, loyalty, and behaved in a much better fashion than the other children.

The other half of the group was given no discipline they got what they wanted, when they wanted it, ran around where they wanted to, and basically had no supervision whatsoever.

There were no spankings out of love, groundings because we care, or direction/guidance of any kind.

This group grew up rebellious, ill mannered, not loving themselves, and even went as far as to say verbally that they wished that someone would spank them or reprimand them so that they felt loved and wanted.

To me that's astonishing that a child at that age would ask to be spanked or have consequences for their actions because they were lonely or felt unloved.

It all goes to prove my point that nothing in life that's worth having will be easy to get.

So it is with May/December romances. They are work, they will challenge you, and they're also extremely satisfying.

My intention here is simply to point out a few facts of younger men loving older women from experience.

Fact one, it may take some time to find the right person so don't get discouraged and give up hope

Fact number two, you're swimming against the grain of society when you choose to make a life with an older woman.

It is accepted for older men to have younger women as wives, but the opposite is unacceptable, another one of those wonderful double standards in our society. So to avoid this becoming too overwhelming, the relationship should be kept off the radar until it becomes a more stable environment. We will talk further on this subject in a later chapter.

It may be weeks or years before you find her. Whatever amount of time it takes, stick it out and you will begin to grow into new and greater things.

Take Maureen and myself for instance, we had to keep ours off the radar when we first met.

Her friends could not have disagreed with her more about what my intentions were when she and I first got together. They thought that I was only after her materialistic valuables, and therefore they wouldn't have anything to do with us.

Over time they began to see that I truly loved her for who she was, wanted to spend the rest of my life with her, and was not after anything that she had of earthly value.

The time span was relatively short for us getting together, however we were on the road traveling for a living which had a dramatic effect on our time frame.

Having materialistic valuables is not a bad thing. However, it should never be a reason for being with someone.

You should be with someone because you feel close to them from spending time together, you feel friendship towards them from developing a closeness of hearts, and you're willing to put aside your differences for the common good of the relationship. Only in compromise does a relationship come to full fruition.

Yet, there are some things that you never compromise such as your loyalties and your values and morals.

So, as you can see, it is definitely a juggling act when you begin your journey towards finding that ultimate someone you can't live without.

It's not for the faint of heart or for those who are easily discouraged. The rewards, like having someone that grounds you, are tremendous.

What I mean by grounding is, she keeps me on a straight and narrow path, not only spiritually but also physically, mentally and psychologically.

She rounds me out if you know what I am saying. I was a little rough around the edges when she met me, but all is well the way it has progressed in our marriage.

Now back to my early 20s, where I was trying to build a career as a glazier/glass technician. I would have been 22 at the time.

I was living in Arizona when I got my first position as a glass technician. The glass business would stay with me for the rest of my life.

I remember a mirror job in Scottsdale, Arizona. The house was worth about $1.2 million. They had ordered a large mirror about 98 inches tall. It was tapered towards the top into a round circle. It was 4 feet wide at the bottom approximately a foot and a half wide at the top. We were installing it above the mantle over the fireplace. It was my first big mirror job.

Come to find out the couple that owned the house where the middle of a divorce. The woman of the House ordered some more mirrors and needed a window repaired that was broken, so I was sent back out to the house the following week.

I performed the necessary repairs/installations and as I was getting ready to leave she asked if I want them iced tea.

Naturally, in Phoenix it was hot, so I accepted. We talked for nearly an hour and she invited me to dinner. She said she just wanted to have some company as she was going through her divorce.

I dated her for several months without telling anyone. I kept off the radar on purpose not only for her, but for me as well.

She told me she had never been with a younger man but that she enjoyed my maturity and honesty.

She would've been 11 or 12 years older than me at the time. She told me that she had kept our relationship off the radar as well, because she was afraid that her family and friends would not understand.

After five or six months I got a phone call that said she and her ex-husband were going to try and work things out, so that was the end of our relationship.

Everything that happens to us in life happens for a reason. I don't know what the reasons were, but I know that it worked out for the best, because shortly after that I started dating the woman that would become my first wife. And that my friends will bring us to the next chapter.

Chapter Three
My First Marriage & Beyond

In the last chapter I began to tell you about my first marriage. Shortly after I had the relationship with the mirror lady, my best friend's wife introduced me to the woman who would become my first wife.

My best friend's wife used to work at the local florist shop which was located less than a mile from where I was living at my mother's house.

One day I was getting some flowers for my mother and one of her friends came in while I was there. While she was buying some flowers, I went up to the counter and whispered in her ear, introduce me to your friend. So she did, which led to she and I starting to date one another.

She was six years older than me. I suspected that when I saw her that's why I asked for the introduction.

I can still smell the scent of the flowers coming from that florist shop. I distinctly remember it being between 2 and 3 p.m. in the afternoon on a Friday. It's funny how the mind remembers the small things.

We talked while she assembled our floral arrangements. The arrangement that I was buying my mother was a special order with rosebuds in it, so it took some extra time, which gave me the opportunity to get her phone number, naturally. Each time I smell that scent I recall meeting her that day.

The mind is a funny thing. It holds on to the smallest of situations. And yet often can't remember what it had for breakfast two days ago ha, ha, ha…

Anyway, we got to know one another and before you know it I had moved in with her and her two kids. One child was 6 and the other was eight.

She and I were together for just short of 9 years. We lived together for the first four years and then got married in the backyard of my mother's house. We were married for nearly 5 years.

Our divorce became final due to a mutual understanding, in 1999. I went on with my life and she went on with hers.

The search for my soul-mate eventually brought me to Florida, Tampa as I recall.

I've always loved to travel, so anywhere in the United States would have been all right with me. I like it all

So I visited 48 of the 50 states as I was growing up and therefore have some experience in traveling.

I started working my airbrush, once again, in order to make a living down in Fort Myers, Florida.

It didn't last long with me, the humidity and high heat in Florida though, especially South Florida, so I headed north where I knew there would be cooler temperatures.

I've always been a person who sweats a lot. So the warmer climates are rough on me. I can handle them it's just nice to have the cooler evenings.

It would turn out later that Florida would play a big role in a large portion of my life.

When I got up north I was looking for a place to set up my airbrush, so I went directly to New York City where I knew I'd find work.

New York is a fun place to work for a while and then leave, but I don't think I'd want to live there on a permanent basis. It's just too crowded for me.

It's a wonderful city. I love New York City, so all you New Yorkers, don't get me wrong. I visit you often. New York City's always been good to me.

So there I was with my airbrush set up to make a living, once again. I've always noticed myself paying more attention the older ladies so it's actually a habit for me to gravitate towards them.

I met several older women while I was working in New York City. I was never much of one to do the dating scene a lot, but I did date a couple of times while I was in New York.

I would take them to restaurants and they would want to pay for the meal. Sometimes I would let them and sometimes I wouldn't. It depended on how insistent she was at the time.

New York women are different than anywhere on the planet. When they have their minds made up its no questions asked.

Dating New York women is an experience I encourage every man reading this to take part in and experience fully.

I find myself drawn to the experiences and the colorful character of older women. They're just different than younger women. Their tastes are different. There turn-offs and turn-on's are different, if you know what I mean? They can carry an intelligent conversation.

It wasn't too long before I found a traveling festival where I could set up my concession trailer every week. I was 28 at this point in my life and it would be four or five more years before I met Maureen.

The traveling life is not for everyone. It can't get rough out there sometimes. No risk no reward. I'm the type of person that enjoys being in a different town every couple weeks all year round. I used to stay on the road with the festivals for 10 or 11 months out of the year. I'm talking 300 days on the road out of 365 days in a year. That's a lot of traveling! But it's something that I enjoyed so it worked for me.

It would be the business where Maureen and I would meet three or four years down the road.

I began traveling all up and down the East Coast of the United States. Each week as I set up my concession trailer for air-brushing hats and T-shirts, there were several older women that would come and talk to me.

Here i was again finding older women. It has a lot to do with the attitude that you portray. What you put out you will get back, so to speak.

I was putting out to the people around me that I was interested in older people. And that's a big clue for all you younger guys looking at older women.

It becomes a way of life. If I were to put out that I like younger women they would be attracted to me, and vice versa.

In my opinion, it comes from within you. No ifs, ands, or buts about it. You choose your own destiny and I chose to pursue older women.

I traveled through Washington, DC, down into Virginia, and all through both of the Carolinas. That year we ended our season in mid-October, the 17th if I remember correctly.

We came to rest in a small-town just south of Tampa called Gibsonton, Florida. It's a place where a lot of entertainment people have their winter homes.

It would be an uneventful winter which would last three or four months till the end of March.

That winter I looked around and talked to a bunch of entertainment people about finding a better festival route.

I would end up with a route that would bring together Maureen's path and mine. Of course it would be two years down the road, but it would be on this route.

Traveling for a living can be very rewarding. It has its ups and downs. One of the rewards is being able to go antiquing in all the different cities and small towns. You learn a lot about culture and history as you travel.

Of course when I was spending time around the Washington, DC area a friend of mine and I visited the Lincoln Memorial and a bunch of the different museums while we were there.

I was particularly taken by the Space and Aeronautics Museum. I would encourage everyone reading this to get to Washington, DC and visit the museums if you ever get a chance.

All the Smithsonian Institutes work in the museums is tremendous Make sure you have plenty of time when you go, as there is a lot to see.

I ended up working in New York City at the stadiums. I worked at Yankee Stadium. I worked at Shea Stadium, and several other small parks around the Queens, Brooklyn, and Bronx areas of the boroughs of New York. Some of them were rough others weren't. All in all I created plenty of cash flow in the New York area.

The Long Island portion of New York is a whole other world. It's over 100 miles long and it has an extremely diverse population, ranging from modest one-bedroom homes to multimillion dollar mansions on the beach. Location is everything, especially on Long Island.

I have worked small street festivals on Long Island that were some of the largest grosses I've ever had. These festivals would start about five or six in the evening and last until two or three in the morning.

There were large beer tents on the streets, so you had to deal with a lot of drunken patrons.

I remember one Friday evening that I grossed $2900 at the Italian street festivals on Long Island. That's a pretty good chunk of money for one nights work.

Of course all the festivals are not like that. The average would be between $500 and $1000 on a good evening, with my art concession.

Every new town was another opportunity for me to meet older women. I have found estate sales, yard sales, flea markets, and the like, to be excellent places to meet older people. So I used these avenues to my advantage while I was traveling.

I used my time on the road to search my own soul in order to find what I was looking for in life. You get a lot of insight into yourself when you see how others live.

Different types of cultures, different types of attitudes and characteristics of individuals from different cities and towns all up and down the East Coast. From Florida to Maine and everything in between, I traveled this area nearly 4 years.

The times of year worked out perfect because we would be in Florida where it's warm for the winter, and by summer we'd be up in the northern part of the country where it is nice and cool.

As I recall it was one of the more enjoyable times when I was single.

I enjoyed the diversity of life for those four years. At which point I was looking for something more in depth and permanent.

These feelings would draw me closer to my soul-mate, although at that time I had no idea that it was happening. Life has a way of closing at one door and then opening a window so you can see where to go.

I've always tried my best to stay positive about life. My positive attitude and yearning for my soul-mate would put me on a collision course with destiny.

Chapter Four
Meeting Maureen

After being on the road for quite some time, I started yearning for something permanent and not so up in the air. Life out on the road is up in the air all the time.

Like constantly waiting for a place to park your house trailer or not knowing if you're going to get a good location for your concession so you can pay your bills that week. These are a few of the things that create the downside to that business.

It was springtime 1998 and I was working at a festival outside of the Raleigh-Durham area of North Carolina. Our next festival would be Greenville, North Carolina.

This little festival would mark a large change my life. Not only would it put me on a path with destiny, it would also bring completion to my soul's yearnings. To say that it was life-changing would be an understatement considering the impact that it had on the rest of my life.

Maureen and I would meet in Greenville North Carolina that year, 1998. The circumstances surrounding our paths crossing are unique and interesting in their own right, so let's start there.

It wasn't a very long drive for me to get from the Raleigh-Durham area where we were working, to our next festival in Greenville, N.C. so I would stay one more night in Durham area and then drive over to Greenville in the morning. I remember finishing the Raleigh-Durham area Festival on Sunday evening. The next morning was a beautiful day for traveling. I slept until nine or 10 in the morning.

I had prepped my trailers for the road the night before, so it was just a matter of getting some breakfast down my neck and hitting the highway.

The trip to Greenville was uneventful, and when you're out on the road driving, uneventful is a good thing.

It would be early to mid-afternoon when I reached Greenville that day. If I recall there were no clouds in the sky. It was a beautiful blue sky for miles in every direction. The sounds of spring were in the air. The birds were chirping. The squirrels were running around gathering for the coming summer. The Carolinas are very woodsy, so there are pine trees everywhere. It's a beautiful part of our country.

The Greenville Festival had a small lot for its location. It was a small area next to the mall in the parking lot.

Some weeks we would be on the actual city fair grounds lot. Other times we would be in a Kmart or Wal-Mart parking lot. Still other times, we would be in a park.

The diversity is what drew me to that business to begin with. How true is the variety of life being its spice to someone who feels as I do?

The traveling and soaking in of the sights, sounds, knowledge and diversity was a major factor to me when I decided to go on the road for a living.

As I was about to find out being on the road would bring to me the love of my life. I could tell this festival wouldn't be very big. You can usually tell by the location of the lot.

This particular lot was close to the Mall in the parking lot, however, "close" is not "at" which brings us back to location, location, location.

Although, I've seen some smaller festivals bring in some pretty hefty grosses. Appearances can be deceiving. You never can tell what a festival is going to be like until you work it.

So it is with people. Appearances can fool you, so don't let them. You don't judge the book by its cover. You read it and come to your own conclusions based on its content.

This is a parallel that can be drawn when you're dealing with people. Don't judge someone by their appearances. Get to know their content and base your conclusions on the facts, rather than on appearances. This way your relationship is based on raw, un-fooled around with truth.

You know them, they know you. Sounds like the only good place to start to me. I waited around the lot to get my location. Then I could set up my concession trailer.

It takes time to get your trailer on location, take off the hitch, open it up and set up all of the equipment & flash so I wanted to do it as quickly as I could. It's an all-day affair, if you know what I mean.

It was late when they gave out locations so I put my concession trailer on its location and called it a night. At that time, I had a small house trailer that I pulled up and down the highway with me, to have some place to live, so I went back to my trailer and crashed for the night.

The next morning would change my life. I couldn't wait for the excitement of getting my concession trailer ready to go to work. There was a strange calm in the air that night. I would understand it much later, but it was quite foreign to me at the time. She would come to me in the morning I got started early the next morning, opening up my concession trailer, prepping my compression tanks, all of the usual set up for one of these festivals.

This is where I tell you that flash equals cash! Once again, appearances, as I said before. The better your concession looks the more money you make, so your flash is very important.

So I made mine look awesome as usual. As I stood there next to my concession I looked around the lot to see who else was setting up.

I saw a group of people I had never seen before until I saw their manager. It turns out that I used to work with their manager on a different festival route.

I caught his glance across the small festival grounds where he was setting up his concessions and called him over.

As we stood there talking I noticed a strong featured older woman with a look of vulnerability in her eye.

This would turn out to be the fact that she was just recently widowed. Not that she was vulnerable by any means, because she's not. You can trust me on that one.

This friend of mine was not the sharpest knife in the drawer, so I had to ask him to introduce us.

As we walked towards her I could see she had on very nice silk shirt with ruffles down both arms. It was purple with a black tuft. She had blonde hair with dark streaks in it. My initial guess of mid-to-late 50s turned out to be a few years off. As my friend began to introduce us I took command of the situation and grabbed her hand and kissed it. It's the only proper thing to do when you're dealing with a classy woman.

This woman had class oozing from every pore. She was bright, intelligent, and in charge of all that was around her.

The first thought I remember running through my head was her stature. She is a short little thing, small and petite. Yet she commands the respect of those around her. I was impressed to say the least.

She looked awestruck when I lifted my sunglasses to reach and kiss her hand.

I recall that look in her eye, it was innocence. Experienced but innocent! I would find out later that this look was because of the intuitive vision she had seen earlier that spring.

It was set up day so our conversation was brief. Everyone comes together for set up so the job can be done quickly and efficiently. It would have to be in the morning.

That's what I would do. I would get out on the festival grounds early the next morning hoping she'd be there.

It was going to be a restless night for me. I was excited at the prospect of meeting an older woman that had class and brains too!

The next morning I got up earlier than usual and headed for the little coffee shop across from the festival grounds.

As I was getting ready to order, guess who walked in, none other than Maureen herself. I asked if she would like to join me for breakfast. Of course she accepted and we had our first meal together. It was a quaint little coffee shop with old-time knickknacks and memorabilia hanging on the walls. I recall it sparked several conversations between us as we both have interests in antiquity. I enjoy small, mom-and-pop operations like that one, in different little towns along the way.

As we sat there enjoying each other company over breakfast I pondered in the back of my mind if it would be to forward of me to ask her to dinner. By the end of the meal I had decided that I wanted to spend more time with her.

I asked her to have dinner with me that evening and she accepted. I told her I'd pick her up around 8 p.m. and take her someplace special.

I hopped in my truck and drove back to where my trailer was parked. I gathered together what I'd need for the day and headed for the festival grounds.

I didn't have much left to do on my concession but I knew that Maureen's crew wasn't finished setting up her concessions. After finishing mine I hung around hoping to catch her not too busy and spend some more time together.

I was strangely drawn to her presence. She was the one I had been looking for.

I still had no idea at this time that she had seen, in her minds eye, our meeting and getting together. She was so captivating to me that I wanted more.

We ended up spending some quality time together that afternoon. It came in short little sessions due to the fact that she kept getting interrupted by her help.

All in all I enjoyed our brief time together. I left the festival grounds mid afternoon and headed back to my trailer to get some rest for the evening. I would sleep for a few hours and then get ready to take her to dinner.

My alarm went off at 7 p.m. I got up and dressed in my best suit. I had made reservations earlier that day at an exquisite little seafood restaurant I had found while driving around town.

She had told me she lived in Florida so I suspected she liked seafood, and I was right. By 7:30 p.m. I was ready to go. It was a small-town so the drive to pick her up wouldn't take but 15 minutes. I arrived to pick her up around 7:45 p.m. I walked her to my car and opened the door for her like any gentleman would. As we drove I explained to her that I had made reservations for us at a nice little seafood restaurant nearby.

This restaurant was something out of a dream. It was elegant, on a private pier and very ornate. They were playing her favorite music when we got there. So I couldn't have worked that one out better if I had tried.

We enjoyed a succulent seafood meal in the dining atmosphere that would melt your blues away. It was a wonderful evening that I won't soon forget.

We shared with one another our likes and dislikes. We both found out that either one of us drinks alcohol. This was a big relief to me as I can't stand being around alcohol. The smell of it turns my stomach inside out. It's a gift I suppose. Just the smell of alcohol makes me want to throw up. I would find out later that her mother was an alcoholic and that was why she didn't drink.

On our drive back to her motel we continued to share with one another our differences and similarities. I said to her I can't quite explain the feeling is that I have right now. I know how much difference there is in our age, but it doesn't matter to me I told her it felt like we had known one another for ever.

I asked her if she truly understood what I was saying, because she had a puzzled look on her face. She proceeded to tell me what she had seen in her mind's eye, the intuitive vision of the blonde haired man with glasses. She told me she felt the same way about knowing me for a long time.

It was a wonderful thing that we both felt the same way. Finally a future that looked bright and exciting.

I walked her up to her motel room, kissed her hand again, said goodnight and went on my way. I had made plans with her to meet for breakfast the next morning. What a wonderful feeling to connect with someone on so many levels.

The beginning of the rest of my life was starting right in front of my eyes. I was taken by surprise at how quickly it all happened.

One day we were acquaintances, the next day we were having an intimate dinner together. How quickly time flies when you're having fun, wouldn't you say?

After breakfast together the next morning we went to the festival grounds. I gave her some suggestions about her concessions.

It's hard to give advice, but especially to someone older. I thought to myself, what could I possibly tell her about this business that she doesn't already know? As it turned out quite a few of my suggestions ended up refining her process and streamlining the operation.

I gave her suggestions on ways to increase her gross and a few other tricks of the trade that I had up my sleeve. I was afraid that we might not see things eye to eye in business.

Not everyone can work together. So it was a trial period for us. It turned out that we were excellent together in business. Between her experience and my new ideas we made excellent partners.

At lunchtime we went and got a hamburger together. I proceeded to tell her of my many skills which include mechanics, sales, inventory, artwork and design, architectural drafting, food management, accounting, writing, and all phases of remodeling homes. My list of knowledge is extensive but it has taken years to get there. After hearing of my extensive knowledge and capabilities she put an offer on the table that at the time couldn't have been better for me. I was struggling with a small operation. So we joined ranks and put our two businesses together. Joining with Maureen was the best move of my life for many, many reasons.

We worked independent of one another for the rest of that festival and things went up from there. We began to take all our lunch breaks together and were spending more & more time together.

It was great to think that I had a best friend once again. Best friends are rare and when they come along you'd better treat them well.

We would be traveling to upstate New York for our next festival. After working together with one another for that festival we decided to simply combine the entire operation and look after it together

I sold my little travel trailer and we used motels to live in. Doubling back to get my house trailer became too much of a burden in gas and that's why I sold it.

I helped her build new cases, counters, and reorganized her concessions. She had up three at the time as I recall.

Combining our businesses turned out to be very beneficial to both operations. Her operation was lacking a leader and I became that for them. Maureen was lacking a large shoulder to lean on and I became that for her. I was looking for a home and for something more permanent so it became that for me.

What a peaceful feeling when your life brings you joy and happiness. Maureen would turn out to be the best thing that ever happened to me.

I was a very lucky man when I met her. Destiny had brought us together, fate would keep us together.

Chapter Five
Getting Together for the First Time

As I looked at our scheduled route it became apparent to me that we had a lot of work ahead of us.

We had a bunch of festivals coming up in New York ranging from Tonawanda, to Oswego, and then on to Buffalo and ending up in Niagara Falls. What a beautiful route. That part of upstate New York is a spectacular part of the Northeast.

We ended up making a very good living that season. When we got to Niagara Falls, which is known as the honeymoon capital of the world, we talked of moving in together.

Up to this point we had been spending the extra money on two rooms for appearance sake. It would be good for us to move in together and see if that part of our relationship was compatible.

I headed into the local town to get some supplies for our operation. While I was running around town I found a perfect little motel just off downtown that would suit my needs to a tee. So I went ahead and rented us a room for the length of the festival. The name of it was honeymoon acres.

Here I was living a dream. Not even realizing all of what was to unfold in my life. Here I had met a wonderful, kind, intelligent, business oriented, compassionate woman. I was ready to embark on the journey of a lifetime.

Ever since we had put our businesses together they began to flourish. They complemented one another so well that it made them both stronger. I began to look at how well she looked after her own operation. This was direct insight into her character so I soaked it all in. She was firm yet kind. She didn't put up with any "B.S." from anybody. I like that strength in a woman. So not only were we becoming close friends but I was beginning to fall for this strong, take charge woman. The first thing that I evaluate when I decide to take on a serious relationship is, how much commitment am I taking on and am I ready for that amount of commitment? So I began to ask these questions of myself. The answer came back quick and concise. Yes!!!

Once I struggled within myself and decided what I wanted to do, I put my whole heart into our operation and our relationship.

So I set my mind and my heart on the route that we had chosen for the year of festivals to work, and we aimed for the sky.

We were at Niagara Falls by this time getting ready for another 10 days of fair time. There was a hustle and bustle in the air as all the concessionaires began to reassemble their operations.

One of the cotton candy wagons had made fresh popcorn and I could smell the buttery fresh flavor of popcorn in the air. As we began our set up operation like everyone else, I turned to Maureen and thanked her for her kindness and her quick thinking, witty attitude.

A lot of the anxiety and stress of being on the road was just lifted off of both of us due to the fact that we had one another. We could now lean on one another in the hard times and, as they say, "have each other's backs".

There are a lot of loud noises on the festival grounds as they begin to set up the big machines that will twirl the kids around in circles for two weeks.

You hear sledgehammers driving stakes in the ground to support the beams for the Giant Wheel, trucks racing everywhere trying to get their loads to their destinations on time, It's a fast-paced life on the road.

We got our operation up and ready, and were ready for the first day of work. Most of our festivals would open on Fridays so Friday, Saturday, Sunday—the first weekend was always exciting.

Friday was slow this particular year, but come to find out the rest of this festival would be very good. So Maureen and I headed back to the motel.

It would be our first night sleeping together in one room. We went and got some coffee and pie because we had eaten earlier at work and wanted some desert.

At a 24 hour coffee shop Maureen and I sat down to relax after a night's work. I asked her if she honestly approved of us moving in together. She paused for a few moments before she answered me with, are you kidding, of course!!!

She has a direct way about her which makes her very straightforward. You can either handle it or not.

So when she answered me it came across to me as, hey buddy, you better catch up!!! It was said in her quick witted, humorous tone which made me laugh at the time. We both enjoyed some humor and headed back to the motel.

The first night was amazing. She and I hit it off like no two people ever hit it off. We were laughing, carrying on and having a good time. We ended up together that night and had such a wonderful evening.

Earlier that evening I had carried her across the threshold as if we were just married.

The room had a Jacuzzi off to one side and a heart-shaped bed on the other. The hot tub helped us both to unwind and relax. As we sat there in the Jacuzzi I massaged her back and arms.

Quick note to all you younger guys, massages work. After our stay in the Jacuzzi we proceeded to the heart-shaped bed where I had put the massage oil in a cup of hot water. Naturally, I had bought her flowers and a card. Quick note to all you younger guys, the flowers and cards work great so use them.

I gently laid her on the bed face down. As I poured the warm oil over her back, she began to groan with relaxation. Oh yes, oh yes she said as I massaged her legs and arms.

Now, because I was raised in a conservative home that's as far as I'm prepared to go with that story.

Suffice it to say I brought her to her ecstasy point many, many times that night and showed her what real love was all about. We let our expressions speak. Our soft touches took us to a place that only comes when you bond with someone. You become one with them.

I remember us both getting hungry about halfway through the night, so we went out and got some Mexican food. We had some deep-fried ice cream, which is one of my favorites, to top the night off. It genuinely was a night to remember.

Saturday and Sunday were both big days at the festival so we would get some sleep.

Saturday and Sunday would end up being very profitable for us. However, it does come at a price, and that price is 15 hour on your feet for two days, back to back. The festival usually opens later during the week, so on Monday you get a reprieve.

Through the week we would occasionally have extra time on our hands. We love to go antiquing, along with seeing the historical sites.

As I recall, we went to the falls several times while we were there in Niagara. This would be one of the more memorable festivals, in my mind.

A quick note to all you younger guys, take her places. Women love to go out to the mall, or grocery shopping, or antiquing for instance, It doesn't matter how old or young they are. Oh yes, do it with some enthusiasm and your response from her will blow your mind. Women see your enthusiasm as a sign that you're paying attention to them, and are actually interested.

This goes a long way towards building a fun based relationship. Isn't that what life is all about anyway, having fun? I mean, seriously, if you don't enjoy what you're doing, why are you doing it?

So I had hit a home run with this one. She was a keeper, if you know what I mean.

We worked the rest of the Niagara Falls Festival. That one will be etched in my memory forever.

Chapter Six
Introducing Maureen to My Family

After working all through New York and the Carolinas we worked some small festivals in Georgia before ending up down in Tampa, Florida that year.

I had received a call from my grandfather two months previous to our season ending.

We would need to store our equipment on the property in Tampa and drive 2500 miles to see my grandmother on her deathbed. On top of that, there was a hurricane bearing down on the west coast of Florida and all the TV stations were running evacuation notices.

So it all worked out for the best as we left Tampa right away that September.

The trip to Colorado was an anxious one for me, worrying about my grandmother. When you've traveled as much as we have, driving 800-1000 miles in one day is commonplace. We made real good time, short of a few tire problems. But that's to be expected when you're pulling trailers.

As we drove across this great country of ours I couldn't help but think to myself how lucky we all are to live in a free society, and to be a part of the greatest nation on this planet.

It was a wonderful feeling to be alive. With our new relationship, we were on the road to greatness.

It was early November so the southern route would not be as hot this time of year.

We wanted to take Interstate 10 all the way to Dallas, Texas and then head north, but the hurricane was headed for the coast so we went further north to Kentucky to get away from it.

We burned up the highway and made real good time. Within 3 1/2 days we were sitting in Grand Junction, Colorado with my grandparents.

Keep in mind, I was raised in this town and went to school here, so I know the city like the back of my hand. It came in handy when I showed Maureen around some of the beautiful mountains, lakes and national parks.

The Colorado River and the Rio Grande River meet in Grand Junction. This is where they got the name Grand Junction. It's the junction of two grand rivers.

Our first weekend there was great because Maureen and I were by ourselves and we got a chance to see some of the sites. However, it wouldn't stay great for long.

After a long counseling session with my grandmothers Dr., I came to the conclusion within myself that I needed to stay there until she passed, In order to help my grandfather with whatever needs he had at the time, as well as for my own closure.

Now, I would have to change my whole plan of attack. It looked like we'd be staying in Grand Junction for a while.

Doctors had given her six months to live, so I didn't know if we would be there for a week or a year. This meant I would have to secure some finances right away, so I went back to the glass trade.

I got a job within a day and was back to work pulling down a weekly paycheck. It would end up being four months before she actually passed on.

It was extremely difficult watching my grandmother lie around expecting to die. No matter what they say you never get used to it.

My mother had that same expectation of death before she died of cancer back in 1991, so I had been through this before. My concern turned toward my grandfather.

117

After her passing he would be all alone and over 80. I wanted to help as much as I could, but nothing helps the grieving process. It has to run its course.

There ended up being a little bit of snowfall that year but not much. It did get below freezing several times, however. This prompted me to wrap our water hose in heat tape so it wouldn't freeze solid. If you've ever lived where it gets below freezing than you understand what I'm saying. It would be similar to your garden hose freezing solid and you not being able to use it.

So we did what we had to in order to survive for the few short months that my grandmother had left on this earth.

The days turned into months and before long we were looking at January.

As I look back now those four months went by very quickly, although they seemed to drag on at the time. Maureen and I spent our extra time with my grandparents.

We had found a small RV park close to my grandparents' house. It was a more conservative little park, with a small amount of tenants. It would be perfect for our needs at that time.

By January my grandmother's health took a turn for the worse. Her doctors would give her permission to come home for a week or two from the hospital, and then she would begin to go downhill again.

Naturally, it would be back to the hospital right away with Grandma. Until the day we got the phone call from my grandfather. Grandma had not made it through the night, she was passed now. It was a relief on one hand, and a strong burden on the other, considering my grandfathers situation, living alone so far away from all his grandchildren.

He was a retired missionary and minister so the church would be a tremendous help in looking after him.

The grandchild closest to Grandpa at that time would have been my oldest sister in El Paso, Texas. Of course, we lived 2500 miles away, so being on hands was out of the question for us.

We would have to communicate with my grandfather by phone. Getting Grandpa through the funeral would be next.

My brothers and sisters and I have never been extremely close. We love one another. However, our lives have taken a myriad of different avenues which have kept us apart in the physical sense. One of my sisters has traveled with her husband in the military for years. My brother ended up out West in the mining industry. My other sister moved around a lot with her husband's job and I was living down in Florida. We were spread all across the United States and had been for years. The time would come when we would all be together again for Grandma's funeral.

The very next morning I got a call from my sister. She explained to me the schedule for the next few days.

There would be a get together with just the four grandchildren one evening another day would be devoted to the memorial ceremonies for Grandma, and still yet another would be dedicated to the actual funeral, the laying to rest of our beloved grandmother.

So as you can see we had a very busy week ahead of us. There would be meetings, introductions, and most of all the reactions from everyone as they were introduced to us. Maureen and I are alike in a lot of ways. One of those ways is neither of us are social butterflies. We would rather stay home and enjoy a good movie and popcorn than to go out dancing and carousing all the time.

My brother and sisters are the opposite. They enjoy going out and painting the town on too often of an occasion for our taste, but that's another whole story in itself.

The introductions would be awkward and yet insightful.

That evening my brother took us all out to dinner at a very nice Italian restaurant. We all ended up having a marvelous evening of laughter, fun and camaraderie.

The first meeting was awkward like I thought it might be, since Maureen and I were not married yet, but were living together.

Remember I said conservative upbringing. Well, my grandfather, as I've mentioned to you, was a retired missionary/minister.

There was no way that we could tell them that we were living together without being married.

Quick thinking Maureen came through for us again. I worked for her as the manager of the operation. It was true, we did not lie. I started out working for her, before she and I got together.

We shared the trailer but not the same bed. Once again we told the truth, even though we had grown past that stage in our relationship, we had been there just weeks before.

All in all Maureen liked my brother best of the three. My oldest sister has always been protective of me since I was young therefore she questioned Maureen extensively on our relationship, hoping to find out what was really going on in order to protect me once again. Naturally, Maureen took this as a frontal assault, as most women would. Maureen and my oldest sister were not compatible but got along fine. My other sister seemed a little stand-off-ish at the time towards us both, as I recall.

I believe it had to do more with her personal relationship at the time, than anything.

When it came to my brother and Maureen, they hit it off huge. They're both very straightforward and both enjoy mild sarcasm, so it was a perfect match.

It always seems that food taste better with good company, so we both enjoyed ourselves, as we had both good food and good company that evening.

The next day would be the memorial services for my grandmother's funeral.

It would be a time of remembrances, weeping, and more fellowship with my family. Maureen and I were growing closer to one another by leaps and bounds.

Our relationship began to blossom after she met my brothers and sisters. It was a relief to me because it told me that she was comfortable with my family.

We had a lifetime of fun and happiness ahead of us. The sky's the limit when you look up.

I remember standing there at my grandmother's grave as if it were yesterday.

The memorial services were held at the church where my grandfather taught on occasions. I still have Grandma's memorial service cards and photographs.

It would be good for Maureen and I to grieve together for the first time. Grieving is a healing process which opens your eyes to a lot of things you normally would never have seen. So it helps you grow and that's what our relationship needed to do at that point.

What a wonderful feeling to know that you're growing towards a greater goal with someone you care about very deeply here was my grandmothers passing drawing Maureen and I closer together, what a complex world we live in.

Friday afternoon we put Grandma in the ground. There were tulips, pansies and an assortment of beautiful flowers at the head of her grave. My grandmother loved flowers and gardening.

I would choose to remember the positive and the good things about my grandmother and draw from their experience towards my own goals.

So here was Grandma's funeral & life, reaching out to change other lives.

We spent time with the family and prepared ourselves for the trip back to Florida. I knew we would want to return to Florida, and resume our business.

We both came away from the experience with insight into one another's character, which was excellent in establishing our relationship.

Once again here is some good advice, learn from your experiences, and take from them what you need for your journey

I have found that older women assist me to better meet my goals, which are met on a much higher level, and more to my satisfaction due to their experience.

Maureen and I enjoy traveling so much, therefore the trip back to Florida would be full of new adventures, in different parts of the country.

Chapter Seven
Getting to Know One Another/
Talk of Marriage

Once you live with someone you begin to know their traits. The funny little quirks come out of the woodwork. That's how relationships grow. The two learn from one another and from their interaction they become one. Hopefully this will help all you young men out there.

I've always been the type for old-fashioned drive-in movies. Low and behold, one of the few drive-ins left in the country is only 10 miles from our house in Ruskin, Florida.

Maureen and I have been down there many, many times over the years. We find more and more things that we have in common, as the years go by.

We are both very much into current events, political views, and news rhetoric. One sign of intelligence is attention to current events. I have found Maureen to be highly intelligent, up to date on political views, and an all-around classy woman.

I enjoy reading as much as she does, although neither of us read as much as we would like to because of time constraints.

Maureen loves to receive cards and letters. She has set of stenographer's pens and knows how to use them well.

She loves to write eulogy cards, dedication cards and that type of thing. It shows me how much he cares about other people, which is a trait that I admire.

Maureen and I would grow together by leaps and bounds over the next year or two. I do my best to get a card and flowers at least once a month flowers and cards go a long way toward showing a woman how much you are thinking about her.

Maureen and I both love to cook. We both love to bake desserts and goodies. This comes in handy on the weekends, because I give her a break from the kitchen and I cook.

There are many other things that we both like. A few of them are antique markets, museums, and seminars. We're the same when it comes to dealing with situations that arise on a daily basis. We deal with them immediately.

We decided we would discuss our differences as they came up, and move on from there. This would strengthen our relationship.

I found myself drawn closer and closer to Maureen by the moment. This is a sign that you've become comfortable around that other person.

When Maureen and I were just getting to know each other at the beginning, she played a bit naive at times to gain my affection. Of course, it worked.

That's what getting to know one another is all about. Compromise, courtesy, and a heart full of love are the three major components to a quality relationship.

Would we travel with our business and work the festivals or find local work and stay in Tampa? Only time would tell. For now, we would get to know one another on a much deeper level.

It wouldn't be long before Maureen and I were talking about tying the knot, making it permanent. This would be a big step for me as I had come out of my first marriage with a different outlook on getting married a second time. It would prove to be different with Maureen, however.

When we got back home, we decided we would go to the justice of the peace in downtown Tampa and make it official. Dear friends of ours stood up for us as witnesses. They took us to a wonderful Victorian style restaurant afterwards.

They gave Maureen a beautiful picture holder for her wedding picture. We still have it on display.

I recall there was a gift shop in the lobby, where I bought some memorabilia for Maureen. What a wonderful time we had with our closest friends that evening.

I took her to an ocean side hotel after dinner, so we could stay on the water. The ocean has a romantic way about it like the wet sand shifting under you or the cool water on your feet. As we sat there that night I realized that I had found my soul-mate.

We would enjoy ourselves that evening, but it was only a precursor to what was to come. I had a huge adventure in store for our honeymoon. We packed up and left for New Orleans, Louisiana the next morning.

New Orleans has always been one of Maureen's favorite places on the planet. I enjoy it myself.

New Orleans is so rich with history it would make a wonderful place for us to start this fantastic journey together.

It's only about 700 miles from Tampa to New Orleans so we would be there in less than a day. It was midday when we arrived, as I recall.

I had known ahead of time that Maureen loved New Orleans, so I planned to take her there several months in advance of us getting married.

I checked us into a French Quarter inn. It had a balcony with an old-time feel to it. Most of that area was built around 1600 to 1700 A.D., and is filled with exciting landmarks, historical monuments and old historical buildings.

I love the cathedrals as you walk towards Jackson Square in downtown New Orleans. Maureen and I stopped at several of them and took our time looking at them.

Another little clue to you younger men out there, spending time together doing things that you both enjoy.

We made our way down to an elegant restaurant. What an exquisite dining experience that was. The steaks were out of this world, and the desert was heavenly. Those are the kind of meals that you never forget, WOW!

The nightlife in New Orleans is so diverse, there is something for everyone. There's country, rock, and last but not least blues. Maureen and I both love the blues, so we had a spectacular time that night listening to the blues bands up and down the strip in the French Quarter.

We never drink alcohol and try to stay away from others that are drinking, however when you're downtown in New Orleans at the blues bars enjoying yourself, it's amazing what you're willing to put up with.

So we had a phenomenal experience that night. We were learning to enjoy each other.

That night rates the highest on my list of sexual encounters. She and I, entangled in one another physically, didn't come up for air until early morning.

The passion that night, along with her being much more relaxed than the first time we were together, were what made it so extra special. We had become one with each other.

I knew in my heart that she was the one for me. We didn't fall in love all at once. Well, she did for the most part, but I didn't. It came gradually over time for me.

I began to respect the way she did business and the way she did pleasure.

We spent a week in heaven exploring all of the sites of New Orleans for our honeymoon. We went to the zoo, the local museums, the old historic sites, and a lot of the blues bars. The week ended too fast of course.

Before I knew it we were staring at another 700 mile trip back to Tampa, Florida. The good things never seem to last long enough, or should I say, they last just long enough.

Life has a funny way of giving you what you need at that moment in time. We had needed the rest, so our honeymoon in New Orleans was a welcome vacation for both of us.

The next morning I ordered breakfast in bed for us. I figured we'd be out of out of town by 9 a.m., putting us in Mobile Alabama for the first night. Now there's a beautiful coastline. Mississippi Alabama coastline is some of the most scenic of that southern route.

We were blessed with beautiful weather for the next day's trip back to Tampa, where I would seek financial income for Maureen I, immediately.

It was less than a day and I went back to work locally. It would be three or four more months before we went back out on the road with our business, so I held down a regular job until then.

We were off to a promising start in this new relationship we had chosen to nurture. We were definitely made for each other. Our lives were entwined by destiny.

Keep looking forward and never give up. Your true love is out there somewhere, waiting for the right circumstances for you to meet them.

Chapter Eight
Our First Years Together

The first problem that is presented to a couple with an Age Gap Relationship is you are both from different eras.

The adjustments will need to come from both sides through compromise.

As we started to settle into our new life together, I began to see that I had made the right choice. Maureen was loving, kind, compassionate, and a whole lot of other things that I need not mention.

First thing I would do for her, would be to help bring her lingerie up to date. This would include sexy new underwear, new sleek looking bra's, hot little dresses and heels, and of course, a new purse or three. Women love to shop for shoes and clothes so naturally she got more than one pair. We bought her belts, scarves, and some cute little outfits to go with them.

It ended up giving her more confidence in her sexual character. We went shopping for these together which in itself drew us closer at the time.

It becomes a commitment on a daily basis, looking after someone who has been given to you by the Angels.

Maureen loves to go with me everywhere. We have become like Siamese twins. As a matter of fact some of her friends call us "the Siamese twins". We love one another's company so much that it works out fantastic for us to be together all the time.

One of my favorite times is our little walks in the evenings. We take our little terrier with us on our walk around the neighborhood. He's like a part of our family, always with us. He loves to travel in our vehicles. As I grow older I am finding that the little things in life make up a large portion of what others expect of us. "Stop and smell the roses", is a common phrase in today's society.

The little things have a way of keeping you young at heart. An example would be driving around the neighborhood at Christmas time to look at the Christmas lights. These types of small gestures are the ones that stay with a person forever.

I see a lot of older people in today's society, who would rather sit home alone then to seek out companionship. They are afraid of what their families might think if they began dating again.

It is truly a sad existence. Loneliness and depression will be the only result.

We were raised in such different environments, that we often bang heads over certain ideas. I have found that communication and honesty solve most of our disputes. We share our feelings, discuss it and then move on.

It seems the longer we're together the more in tune we become with each other's differences. It also teaches you a lot about your own self.

We traveled with our business up and down the East Coast of the United States. We were home for 3-4 months in the winter, and then back out on the road in the spring.

Being up north in the hot summer months was a welcome change from the heat of Florida. On the other hand we were in Florida where it was warm for the winter, so we have the best of both worlds.

Getting all of our equipment ready to go out on the road is a big job. We would have our workers start checking wheel bearings, fluids, hoses, belts, tires, and everything else, on each vehicle that was pertinent to a long trip. This would begin 2-3 weeks previous to actually leaving Tampa. It becomes a way of life working on the road. It's a spirit within you that makes you want to travel. It's common in today's society with all of our transportation technologies. The car of tomorrow will be a hovercraft that does 350 mph above rush-hour traffic. Won't that bring a feeling of safety? Ha, ha, ha.

Flying is one of our more enjoyable things to do. We would love to see the "seven wonders of the world". This would require several long airplane rides.

We quite possibly could end up doing some extensive traveling with our writing. All types of travel are welcome to both of us.

Maureen and I both have a love of blues music. We both love old Ragtime, Dixieland, country, and just good old blues. Sometimes we listen to old rock "n roll or classical. Music has brought us closer.

Going to concerts, parks, outings and special events have brought us to a point of understanding one another's character. It takes you to a deeper understanding of the person that you've chosen to spend your life with.

Another one of our common likes is our love of food. We are both very good cooks. My mother and stepfather owned a restaurant when I was younger. I would work as a glass installer during the day, and then go to the restaurant and help Mom and Dad for the night shift.

It was a good experience for me to deal with the public at a young age. It teaches good social skills. Although I'm not a very social person my social skills are quite adept.

Maureen is not an extremely social person either. This is one of our other common characteristics.

Our love for animals and has brought several cats and one dog into our life since we got together. We have several feral cats in our neighborhood that my wife has a soft spot for. She feeds them every day, which brings them back the next day.

Sometimes they bring friends with them and now we're up to four outdoor cats and three indoor cats. The outdoor cats are no problem as we just feed them. The indoor cats we keep veterinary and vaccination records for, the outdoor ones we do not.

Eventually we would like to have a small ranch with horses, goats, sheep and possibly some alpacas or lamas. This would fulfill a portion of both our dreams.

Our love of traveling is yet another one of our togetherness journeys. Not only did we meet on the road but we have worked together on the road for going on six years now.

Our lives were about to change. Little did we know that after all these years working on the road, we would be staged in Tampa permanently, all year-round.

This would mean our whole world would be shaken up. Would we sell all of our equipment, or just some of it? Would we keep our 40 foot RV or trade it on something else? Where would I decide to work? What path would my career take if we were not working on the road anymore? Would I be able to find a job that both of us could work at or what Maureen be stuck at home all day? Would staying home all the time be too boring for us both?

We could both feel it coming, but we didn't know exactly when it would happen. Being out on the road as a business was not feasible anymore.

The financial profit margin had dropped to a point where we were forced to choose another avenue/career. Maureen and I had been out on the road together for five plus years at this point.

It would not be easy for us to change our entire life structure. We would pull together and make it work out. We are both survivors as well.

In 2004 we had the toughest year financially that we had ever had. It was so bad out on the road that year that I couldn't keep up with my regular payments.

By the end of the year we were no further ahead than when we'd left Tampa in the spring. This would prove to be the straw that broke the camel's back, so to speak.

We had started off the year 2004 in Puerto Rico. In December of 2003 we accepted a job offer in San Juan Puerto Rico we would be down there until the end of February. For 90 days we were in seven different cities on the island of Puerto Rico.

The Caribbean is beautiful that time of year. There were a lot of tourist sites but we were extremely busy and didn't get to most of them.

We would like to go down there in the future and spend some time touring the island as opposed to working it.

They have an attraction in Puerto Rico of Gilligan's Island. All of the Gilligan's Island programs were filmed on this one little island off the coast of Puerto Rico. Plus there were many other tourist attractions we would like to visit someday.

After getting all of our equipment back from Puerto Rico we headed north to the Carolinas. This year would turn out to be the worst year on record for us.

It was one of those years where nothing seemed to work out properly for anyone. No one else was in any better position financially than we were. The festival business was coming to a fast halt.

By the end of the year 2004 we were at our wits end. We would have to make some drastic changes and restructure our business. It would be a long hard road to change.

However, our relationship was strong and vibrant after the first five years and I knew that our future was bright regardless of what we put our mind to. We would overcome this tough situation as we had all the others in years past. When we arrived in Tampa that winter I found a job in the glass industry immediately. We would start there and work our way up to something better. We could not have known how much better at that time. We were both in for a wonderful surprise.

The road ahead looked bright and clear. Once again Maureen and I would go into survival mode and draw strength from one another. Our future looked bright. We had adapted and overcome together.

Learning to use one another's strengths and cover for one another's weaknesses becomes second nature. You begin to work as a well oiled machine.

We can look at one another and often times tell what the other is thinking at the time. It's such a joy and peace of mind when you grow close to someone as we have. I look forward to future.

The years taking care of and looking after Maureen will be a joy for me because I love her so much.

I have found that special someone and have nurtured a loving relationship based on loyalty and honesty. We will continue to grow closer as the years go by.

One thing I would like to say to all you young men reading this is, it takes time and effort to nurture a fun, loving, cherished relationship.

If you're looking for a fast fix then this is not the road for you. However, if you're looking for something worth having and worth putting your effort into then an older woman relationship is just what the doctor ordered for you.

It takes a lot of work but it provides a lot of rewards. Good luck!!!

Chapter Nine
The Good Times/The Tough Times

One aspect of our lives had come to an end. Maureen and I would embark on some brand-new adventures.

Our little home in Gibsonton, Florida is yet another example of our commonalities. It has a pot belly stove with a country motif throughout.

We use the stove for heat in the winters. The one small stove heats the entire house. We have so much fun sitting around watching the fire in the stove when it's cold outside.

There is 35 years of Maureen's collectibles inside our home in Florida. It's as close to being in the country as you can get.

We own a half acre of land along with it. Eventually we would like to plant thick, lavish gardens on 90% of the property. The other 10% would be driveway naturally.

We have full hook ups for our RV out front which basically gives us two homes.

We have a very good life together along with a lot of good times.

It was now 2004 and I had begun to advertise our concession equipment for sale. We would not be going back out of the road therefore we would not need the equipment. We would keep our 40 foot RV. The rest of the equipment had to go immediately.

It would all sell at the end of the year. I had several calls but no takers until November. We would finally make that big leap of faith. We would now trust Tampa to provide a living for us.

So as it stands we have now collaborated for four years on this book what a wonderful time it has been to work with Maureen on a project that could potentially change thousands of lives.

I have been a writer for years and so has Maureen. I have the rough draft for several children's books already done. So this is like living my dream working with Maureen.

When you and your mate enjoy doing the same thing it makes life so much easier. My advice to you here would be to spend time with that special person so you can learn more about them. Knowing their little quirks helps you to better understand if their character is compatible with yours.

If you think about it, your happiness is what's at stake here. You should take plenty of time to search yourself and the other person. This will bring you to a fuller understanding of yourself and what you truly want to bring into your life. You must know beyond a shadow of a doubt that you are ready for this full-time commitment.

Life is full of joy but it generally doesn't come looking for you, you have to make it happen. Life truly is what you make of it.

In my humble opinion societies ideals on age gap relationships is quite frankly ludicrous. It's okay for a man in his 70s or 80s to take for his bride a 20 or 30 year old woman. However, God forbid if an older woman were to take a younger man as her mate.

The double standard here is evident and ridiculous. I have not only been attracted to older women my entire life, but I am married to a woman currently that is 29 years of greater dignity than me.

We get along better than most couples that I see in today's society. We've always been there for one another since the beginning. I lift her up and she lifts me up. Isn't that true love? Or were my parents and grandparents wrong also. They were there for one another as well. This is where I draw my example from, their lives.

It's a powerful feeling to know that you have someone not only standing by your side but they have your back as well. Through thick and thin, through good and bad times we will continue to grow towards one another. We hope that our example will set a new standard for age gap relationships.

Here we were changing careers again. Life has a funny way of throwing curveballs at you however I've never known a curveball to be followed by another curveball.

The point from me to you is, keep your chin held high, pick yourself up and go on. Life will allow you to rebound but you have to want it. So we did, we rebounded we went on with our lives in different careers.

For the first couple of years it was a tough adjusting to staying put as opposed to traveling all the time. It's almost a home sick feeling, a longing for a road to travel. I compare it to a chocolate lovers craving for chocolate. We love to travel.

Our daily routine was nothing short of jam packed. Every day we work between 10 and 14 hours. We had to in order to substantiate the fact that we could live off the road. It's been almost 4 years now that we've been off the road. I suppose that's substantial enough.

I am a licensed Florida trapper, which means I live cage trap animals and then release them in the wild where they are not a threat to humans. It can be a demanding job wrestling alligators but I enjoy the diversity of it. It's a different job every day. One day I'll be chasing armadillos, then the next day I'll be chasing raccoons and opossums.

I also do home repair and remodeling which coincides with sealing up homes from animal damage. It also gives us money on the side for our savings.

Two years went by before we knew it and it was 2006. There was quite a bit of anxiety for both of us during those first couple of years. The urge to travel was very strong but we managed and life has given us time to slow down and write this book.

It's amazing how life knows what you need more then you know what you need.

We worked in the service industry trapping animals. I did all the physical work and Maureen would do all the paperwork and schedule the appointments. We worked as a team and it worked out fantastic. We really enjoyed being together and working with one another.

I couldn't have known what lie ahead of us, tough times with good times to follow. We are over comers because when the going gets tough we get going.

Christmas 2005 was a joyous season for us. We had all the lights on our house lit up. We had a small Christmas tree in the yard, and a large one in the house. Christmas time is a special time for Maureen and I, because it brings us closer together.

It seems that during the holidays we begin to reflect on our lives, giving us a chance to re-evaluate our choices for the future. Reflection is a step towards growth.

2006 started fresh and new like all the years before it. By February/March the trapping business had taken a nosedive financially. I began to look for another source of income. I had to keep the weekly checks coming in. Long enough for us to finish the book and take the next step in our set of goals.

It sure is heavenly how precious little, baby puppies look into your eyes and draw your heart towards them. We were in for a surprise one-day as we exited the freeway north of Tampa.

Out from the bushes jumped an eight week old terrier Chihuahua mix puppy. He was light brown with a white chest and he looked so scared running out of the bushes towards the freeway off-ramp. I pulled over immediately and ran and scooped him up in my arm. He has been our companion ever since.

Naturally, we took him to the veterinarian for a checkup immediately. The veterinarian told us that animals that have been abandoned never get over it. They hold on to the abandonment forever. For this reason he is that much more special to us.

Maureen named him Spirit. He is very spunky and full of spirit, hence the name. It would turn out that Maureen would need a companion for the change that was coming in our lives.

In late March, early April 2006 Maureen had to go to the hospital. It turned out that she would need a stint put in her carotid artery. She was only in the hospital for three or four days.

It was a big scare for me because I know her medical history. Not only has she had to recover from a quadruple bypass she is also a diabetic. Because of these two conditions my concerns for her health were tremendous. Without a doubt that was one of the toughest times for me in our relationship.

It was hard being away from her while she was in the hospital. If you recall they called us the Siamese twins for a reason. This is one of the few times that we would spend apart since we had been together. When you love someone as strongly as I loved Maureen, you feel their pain.

Thank the good Lord for medical technology. She was out in three or four days, and we were on the road to recovery. She is extremely strong for her age. She's very determined and strong-willed. This was a good combination for her to overcome her illness.

After six months Maureen had recovered completely. She was back to her old self in a few weeks but her strength took a while to come back this time.

I was steady at work up at the ranch in North Tampa. As it turns out I am still employed at the ranch to this day.

We made it through another hot summer and prepared ourselves for another winter.

The winters in Florida are mild, to say the least. The temperature never gets below 38 to 40° and it never gets hotter than 65 or 70°. We love to winter in Florida. We would like to purchase a summer home up North to avoid the heat of summer, however. It will all come in good time to those who stand strong and stick it out.

We decorated our little house for Christmas again this year. We enjoy fixing up our little home. That is another one of our common points.

Maureen and I have grown together at a tremendous pace. Our relationship of eight years is the most substantial thing I've ever had in my life. "Till death do us part" has taken on an entirely new meaning for me. I know that we will be together till the end.

We still go on our evening walks around the neighborhood. We take our little dog Spirit with us every time. Like most dogs he loves to go for walks. He has been a true companion for Maureen now that I work at the ranch. She is at the house by herself a lot of the times. Spirit has given her some purpose and meaning in life.

Maureen's eyesight has deteriorated over the past few years. It's hard for her to see the smaller print now. She has had to give up her driver's license and her world has become quite small. She is extremely strong though. She will adapt and overcome and our relationship will grow through it all.

CPSIA information can be obtained at www.ICGtesting.com
Printed in the USA
LVOW12s1327260114

371022LV00002B/175/P